Lily and Me
in
Haut de Cagnes

by
Delaney Henderson

A-Argus Better Book Publishers, LLC

For information:
A-Argus Better Book Publishers, LLC
9001 Ridge Hill Street
Kernersville, North Carolina 27285
www.a-argusbooks.com

ISBN: 978-0-6158586-1-6
ISBN: 0-6158586-1-9

Book Cover designed by Dubya

Printed in the United States of America

Chapter 1

My mother and I were eating in an Indian restaurant, and it was very elegant. There were white table clothes and silver, and a waiter in a white coat and bow tie who took our order. He bowed ever so slightly to Lily—my mother—then smiled at me. Lily had chosen this restaurant after complaining at length about the English food. We had been in London for a just a few days eating bad food. It was 1966, and I was thirteen years old traveling with my mother in Europe.

She ordered curry for both of us. I was feeling right in the world that night and happy sitting in the soft light of the restaurant. The glow of soft lamps reflected off the silver, polished to perfection, and the glasses of ice and water glinted and sparkled. We had gone shopping at Harrods earlier in the day, and my mother had bought me a twill riding coat and leather boots. My new purchases were on my mind.

"Do you want mild, medium, or hot?" the waiter said, and Lily said medium for her and mild for me, knowing it was my first time eating curry. I felt safe and loved then; I was living in a world full of new sensations and things to see and I was ready to try them. I watched my mother eat her curry, and I ate mine, and my world was complete as I ate dinner with her. I had everything I needed or wanted right there, with just the two of us sitting at the table eating curry in the Indian restaurant in London.

When we finished the curry we had sweet orange-colored melon for dessert, from North Africa the waiter said, a fruit I had never tasted before and it was ripe and delicious. I thought about North Africa, that it was an exotic place, and imagined a freighter steaming across the Atlantic full of melons. I watched my mother drink a cup of coffee after we ate the melon. She looked as if she had something on her mind, like perhaps she wanted something other than what was there at the table. Then I realized as I watched her that she wasn't completely satisfied with our dinner and our travels and being with just me. I felt a stab of doubt. We had left California for an extended trip to Europe and it wasn't going to be enough. She was dissatisfied.

We went back to the hotel, and later that night my mother went out on the town on her own, leaving me alone in the room. I lay in bed in the dark, in the London bed and breakfast. Dim light filtered into the room through the curtains, and headlights flickered against the walls as I listened to the sound of cars on the street. I couldn't sleep. A slow realization came to me that I was alone in a strange city, and I then I wondered if I would be able to take care of myself if my mother didn't come back. A lonely fear overtook me, and it was something I had never felt before. The room took on a vaguely threatening aura, its corners menacing. *She might not make it back to the room,* I thought, *and then what? What would I do? Would the man who ran the hotel help me?*

She did make it back with a bottle of wine and plastic cups, and she woke me up from the fitful half-sleep. I sat up against the pillows and headboard, feeling a rush of relief and watched her to pour herself a drink at the table.

"Where did you go?" I asked.

"I went to a pub," Lily said. Her voice was slurred; it a voice I was familiar with and my heart shrank. She sounded cross. She was focused on trying to get the cup out of its wrapping and didn't want to be questioned.

"Did you have fun?"

"It wasn't so great." Something had gone wrong.

"What happened?"

She stopped fussing with the cups and said, "They were rude to me, so I decided to come back here." All of a sudden she looked like she wanted to cry.

"Who?"

"I went to a pub. They were rude to me at the pub."

They hadn't treated her right. Here we had traveled all this way to London, and they hadn't treated her right.

"They asked me to leave, so I went to the store and bought a bottle of wine," My mother said. She started rustling with the plastic wrapper on the cups again; she was having a hard time getting a cup out.

"Oh."

"They don't like Americans," She said.

I watched my mother as she finally yanked the plastic off the cups and set a cup down on the table. Then she pulled the bottle of wine out of a brown paper bag.

"Not very elegant," she said, looking at me, and it must have occurred to her right then that there might be something inappropriate about the scene.

I thought about her sitting in a pub and getting drunk, and suspected the people in the pub most likely didn't like her being there, because when she got drunk she was unpleasant. She was an unpleasant American drunk, and it was completely understandable to me that they would ask her to leave. I didn't say anything. I felt bad for her, it ending that way, her not having a fun night out, and watched as she started to uncork the bottle with a corkscrew. My sympathy evaporated and I felt trapped; I was stuck in this room with her drinking.

I remembered how scared I was that she might not come back, and thought again about her in the pub, drinking alone in a strange city that wasn't welcoming, and the anxious feeling came back.

"I got scared here alone," I said.

"You did?"

"What if something happened to you? There's no one else here to take care of me," I said. I was sitting upright in the bed now, my posture rigid, and my voice sounded shrill.

"Nothing is going to happen," Lily said.

"But what if something did?" I said. My voice was high pitched and insistent, I was upset and startled Lily. She stopped uncorking the bottle and looked at me.

"Dad's not here, only you. What if something were to happen?" I said in the same insistent voice. I could see it was having an effect on her.

"You're worried because your father's not here?"

I nodded solemnly. "Yes."

"Suzanne, I'm sorry. I won't do it again," Lily said. "I won't leave you alone."

"You won't?"

"No, I won't. Now go to sleep." Lily wanted to get back to drinking and started in with the corkscrew and bottle again. The conversation was over.

I fell silent and watched my mother, recognizing the familiar look of drunkenness taking over her features as she drank, her face becoming gradually askew as if it was melting sideways into deformity. It was like watching a car wreck, something you really didn't want to see but couldn't take your eyes off. I felt relieved that I wasn't alone and glad that she was there, but I was trapped. Trapped in a room of saggy double beds covered by nubby bedspreads, with walls covered by dark-green flowery wallpaper. They felt so close those walls, with windows covered by heavy curtains muffling the sound of traffic from a London street. My eyes slid away from my mother and over to the basin and faucet in the corner wash, and suddenly it looked shabby. My mother sat drinking at a wooden table, with her plastic cups and wine, deep in her ruminations, sitting across from me on the bed.

"Go to sleep," she said, and I sank down, drifting, thinking about the first night we arrived.

\

***

Lily had said, "Just take a short walk and come back."

I went on my own, in the dress I had flown in, my long, blonde hair falling down on my shoulders, bare-legged and wearing a three-quarter-length baggy corduroy coat. I had walked briskly into the night with my hands stuffed into the pockets of my coat feeling like I was walking into my future, and it was sure to be grand, and impossible to know.

There was just a smattering of people in Trafalgar Square, Londoners walking to and fro going about their business, and knots of tourists standing in small groups or moving slowly down the street. I was able to pick out the Americans; they were fatter and badly dressed, and it had embarrassed me to be able to pick them out so easily. After all, I was American. I thought they looked foolish.

I had stopped in front of a fountain in the center of the square. There was a tall column in the middle and a crouching lion. I'd seen pictures of this fountain before, but it was nothing compared to actually being there and seeing the real thing. My body was tense with jet lag—we had just arrived—and I felt exultant; the world was new and full of discovery. Great things were possible!

On the other side of the fountain was the National Gallery, a tall and stately building with a façade buttressed by impressive columns. It seemed to have an authenticity that I was beholding for the first time, as if it was the source of things beginning. Yes, that was the way to describe what I had felt. I was at the source of things, and buildings like this in America were imitations, mere knock offs. Here, I was at the crossroads of the past, and I had turned and saw a group of young people dressed in mod clothes gathered in the center of the square, the future as well! It was 1966.

I had glided away, moving gracefully down the sidewalk, a little wary of the people around me; after all, they were all strangers and I was alone. Lily had been too tired to come with me, and she had collapsed in the hotel. I could barely believe that I was there, in London, walking around Trafalgar Square. I had stopped and watched the little cars going around the fountain, on the roundabout. It just seemed plain odd that they were driving on the right side of the car. I got lost in the sounds of the city as I watched and listened to the cars and drivers. Then, snapping out of my reverie, I abruptly turned around and hurried back to my mother. I hadn't made it very far. It was too exciting and I just had to report back to my mother.

I had to share all this with someone.

"You should have been there!" I had said to her, once back in the room. "They sit on the right when they drive, and the cars! They are so little, and there is a lion statue in the fountain."

Lily had laughed, then opened up her guide-book. "It's a famous statue," she said.

"It is?" Of course it was! How could it not be?

"The Land Seer Lion," Lily said.

"Land Seer Lion," I said, repeating the phrase, liking the sound of it. I said it slowly, the words rolling off my tongue.

Lily nodded. "Yes."

"You should have been there and seen it! Let's go now and see it—"

"I'll see it tomorrow."

"Oh, you should see it tonight! Let's go out! Don't you want to go out?" It was incomprehensible that she wouldn't want to go out right now. It was unimaginable to travel so far and arrive and then stay in the hotel room and not go out, and wait until tomorrow. How could anyone wait?

"It'll be there tomorrow," Lily said. "I'm too tired. Now go to bed."

I looked at my mother, assessing the possibility of her changing her mind.

"Tomorrow," Lily said, her eyes already closing, a small smile playing across her face. She was happy to have me with her, I could tell. I relented and relaxed. I could see she wasn't going anywhere, and I was happy to be there with her in the beautiful room with London waiting. I could still feel the sensation of the wood on my hand, as I slid my hand along the wooden banister as we walked up the staircase, curving around and up to this room on the second floor of this grand hotel, alternately gripping the wood and letting it go, grabbing hold of this place to make sure it was real. A crystal chandelier hung down from above the staircase, illuminating the lobby in an aura of elegant grandeur, and my footfalls were soft silent on thick carpets. It didn't last; we had to save money and we moved out the next day.

That was our first night in London.

Chapter 2

The next day, our host at the bed and breakfast took an unusually keen and somewhat disapproving interest in us. He knew Lily had gone out and left me alone in the room. He was a short, stocky man in his early forties, dressed in slacks and a cardigan sweater over a white shirt and tie, with slicked-back, black hair. He spoke with a thick working-class British accent.

He watched as I dug into a greasy meal of fried eggs and bacon, white toast with jam, and black tea. Lily picked at a piece of toast and sipped her tea. She took a small sip of it, then put the cup down.

"You don't like it?" he said, sounding offended. "You aren't hungry?"

"Not so much this morning," Lily said. "I usually drink coffee."

"You went out last night?" he asked.

Lily paused and looked at him, but she didn't answer.

"So where have you been going?" he said.

Lily reported that we had been to the National Gallery and the changing of the Guard, and that we had taken a riverboat up the Thames and that today we would be going to Hyde Park. Then she perked up and went into a monologue, talking at length about Hyde Park, and it was obvious that she thought it was an utterly marvelous phenomenon, that eccentric men stood on boxes and orated on inane topics.... The host listened politely.

Then he said, "There's too many blacks there in Hyde Park. Talking all that nonsense."

I stopped eating and looked up from my thick delicious bacon and messy fried eggs, and stared his beady, black eyes. I noticed a faint odor of hair gel mixed in with the bacon smell as he paced around the room closer to where I sat. He seemed agitated as he circled around the table behind us.

I kept silent and went on eating while watching my mother from the corner of my eye. She was staring down at the table. She looked sick and was hung-over, and maybe she was surprised. Lily was from Texas, and perhaps she thought that this kind of racial prejudice was something uniquely American. Perhaps she had the idea that somehow Europeans were above and beyond it, or maybe it was me who thought this, I was surprised by this ugly talk.

"They're ruining the country, they are," the man continued. "And they keep bringing them in. They keep letting them in."

I stopped eating again and looked at him. Suddenly, he seemed crass.

"You have a lot of blacks there, do you?" he continued on, shaking his head back and forth, encouraged by my mother's silence. He was either spoiling for a fight, or just didn't know when to quit.

"You must know what I'm talking about," he said.

Lily turned and checked to see if I was finished eating. Then she said with a concerted effort, "That kind of talk is hateful. And I don't want you talking like that around my daughter." Her voice was soft and emphatic, but I could tell she was really not up for a battle.

"Finish up, let's get going," she said to me.

"OH! That's what you think, do you? You left your daughter alone up there last night and went out on your own drinking?" he pounced.

"What? It's none of your business where I go—"

"If you leave her up there alone it's my business! We'll be leaving tomorrow," Lily said and got up.

"I think that's best."

It happened really quickly, this final exchange of words, and then we were out on the street, standing in the weak English sun on the sidewalk.

"That was awful. Those things he said are awful."

"Why didn't you say something sooner?"

"I wanted you to finish eating before I said anything," Lily said.

I looked into my mother's face, grateful that she had.

"Let's not let him ruin our day," Lily said. "Don't pay any attention to that man.

We're going to Hyde Park."

I nodded okay, for despite the bad start I was ready for things to take a turn for the better. That was how it went when you were traveling; you took the bad with the good and the good generally won out due to the excitement of the new and unexpected. I was ready to move on and enjoy the day, but we couldn't shake it. Lily's hangover and the nasty exchange stayed with us that day in the park.

We stood and watched men on the soapboxes talking to the wind, talking to whoever would stand and listen, waving their arms and shouting, men who looked as if they lived in poverty, and the words of the host came back to me "a lot of nonsense," and the whole thing didn't seem quite so wonderful as Lily had described it, but instead sad. He had ruined it.

We wandered into Hyde Park, and my mother snapped photos of me, and I snapped photos of her, recording the day, images of my mother who looked sick and hung-over, and slumped in her green suede jacket that had already lost its shape and hung limply on her frame. Looking back, I look anxious and strained in those photos, with worry written of my face.

Chapter 3

Lily and I were on a bus traveling in France along the main highway that stretched along the Cote D'Azur, going from Nice toward Antibes at the far end of the bay. I was tired from traveling, tired from worry, and leaned my head on the windowpane looking out at the sea.

"There's no beach. It's rocks," I said, while mulling over my impressions of Nice. It held a special place in both our hearts, for I had been born here. We passed by the hospital where I was born, and Lily told me I had been born in the midst of great festivities. It had been Bastille Day, and the whole city was celebrating, but Bastille Day was a full month before my birth and the timing didn't make sense. I wasn't impressed with the city. In its shabby elegance, 1966 Nice reminded me of some old dowager lady clinging onto the memory of glory days past. The streets were empty except for working class men at corner bars sucking on cigarettes dressed in blue work clothes. The beaches were empty.

I saw disappointment on my mother's face, and I could tell she felt the same way that I did and it wasn't as she remembered it.

"It was Bastille Day when you were born—there was confetti coming down—"

"Uh huh." I closed my eyes for a minute, thinking about our arrival in France and the past couple of days.

We had walked the Champs Elysees the first day we arrived in Paris and looking up at the sky through the fluttering green leaves of trees and then back down at the shops, I was exultant the world was at my feet. Paris was light and airy after the gloom of London, and the two of us relaxed and seemed to literally exhale and our breathing become easier. We didn't buy anything that first day on the boulevard; we just window shopped. The Champs of Elysees had row upon row of high-end shops, but my mother didn't want to overspend. We had to be frugal, especially after the splurge at Harrods in London. For three days we toured the city. We went to the Louvre to see the Mona Lisa and to see the statue of David, we took a boat down the River Seine, and we visited the Cathedral of Notre Dame. We ate raw oysters in a bistro with large plate-glass windows and watched the fattest man I had ever laid eyes on working his way through a three-tiered platter of cheese and cold cuts.

"Poor man," My mother had said and indeed he was a sorry sight, sitting alone and gorging. On the third day in France, she had gone out drinking and left me in the hotel alone. Why always on day three? Coincidence? That time she had checked with me first and I reluctantly agreed. What was I going to say? No? I wasn't happy about it, but I accepted it. At least I wasn't afraid that time; we were staying in a hotel run by a motherly French woman whose warmth reassured me and I felt safer. The next day, Lily had announced that we were going to the South of France and she was suddenly in a hurry to get there.

"We'll take the high speed rail . . ." she said, and launched into a lecture about the merits of the high speed rail and how the US was sorely lacking and behind in this area of public transportation.

We had wheeled our large suitcases into the train station and sat on a bench by the tracks. My mother was agitated and hung over, and I was quiet, being careful to not to aggravate her any further. A train was stopped directly in front of us, and people boarded it intermittently with the station agent going about his business of checking and punching their tickets. After watching this for a few minutes, Lily had asked him for tickets, and he refused to sell her tickets. They had gotten into an argument in half French, half English that was incomprehensible to me and everyone. I watched this exchange uneasily, and then finally the station agent shrugged in that way the French do when exasperated and turned his back to her and stalked down the platform, muttering. My mother watched his receding figure and became indignant.

"How rude! He won't sell us tickets!" Her face was red and puffy looking.

I looked at my mother. "Maybe it's not the right train," I said pointedly. The conductor turned around, looked back at me, and nodded empathically.

"Don't pay attention to him!" Lily said. "He's just being rude and won't sell us tickets."

The train whistle blew. "Let's go! We'll miss the train!" My mother had said. "We'll buy our tickets on board." She got on the train, dragging her suitcase up behind her.

"No! Madam, No!" The station agent rushed back over and shook his head emphatically from the platform.

"Mom! It's not the right train! Mom!"

"C'mon! Come on!" Lily was onboard and had found a seat. Now she was waving out the window to me. "Get on board!"

I looked at the station agent, who was shaking his head, and the train blew its whistle again. I had to make a choice: Either get on the train with my mother or be left behind. I looked around the cavernous train station, imagining what it would be like to be alone and left behind and became unnerved. I dragged my suitcase up the metal steps onto the train, and I took a seat next to my mother on a slatted wooden bench.

"The nerve of that man!" Lily had said.

I looked around the compartment. It was full of French peasants, or what I perceived as French peasants, and they might not have been from France at all but from Belgium as it turned out, and perhaps not peasants at all. Some had clucking chickens in wooden crates placed next to them on the bench or were holding the crates on their laps. Some had packed elaborate picnic lunches that they were already starting to unwrap.

"I don't think this is the right train," I said.

"Don't be so negative!" My mother was sharp. "Of course it's the right train."

We sat side by side on the hard bench, and I looked around at my fellow travelers with curiosity—an old woman swaddled in black with crates, and old, wizened men in caps, smoking pipes.

The train traveled north into the countryside, stopping at small villages as it went along, moving slowly, and disgorging passengers as it went, a few at a time. Hours passed. The train seemed to be slowing as it moved through the countryside, stopping and then starting.

"We're almost there," Lily said.

She looked worried; most of the passengers were off the train. I glanced at her. I was getting angry and I was hungry; we'd been watching people eat their picnics.

Finally, all the other passengers had gotten off the train, and we were the only ones left. I watched as the last passengers got off in front of a small, gray building in bucolic green-rolling countryside.

"We should get off," I said.

"We're not there yet," Lily said.

The train went off the main track and came to a shuddering halt.

"The train is stopped," I said. I craned my neck, looking back at the station. "That was the last station."

Reluctantly, my mother got up from the seat where she had sitting rigidly for the entire trip, with upright posture and her back completely strait, barely moving a muscle. She moved to the front of the train and poked her head out the open door. She looked down the long platform at the small building back in the distance.

I stood up and looked out the window on the opposite side of the car. "The train is off the tracks!" I said in disbelief. We'd gone off onto a dead-end side track.

My mother came over to where I stood and looked. "You're right," she said, then sighed. She was resigned, she was beat.

"I'm sorry, I'm really sorry." She went back to the other side of the train and looked at the platform, assessing the situation.

"We'll have to walk back. Let's get off," she said.

Mollified, quiet and sobered up, Lily clambered down off the train, dragging her suitcase behind her with me in tow, and the two of us wheeled our suitcases back down the long platform to a small stone building, the last train station. I was angry.

When we entered the station, we stepped into a bar and a restaurant that was bustling with customers. Everyone looked up at us in surprise. We stood there self-consciously, and the room became quiet for moments. Then they politely looked away, and someone muttered something unintelligible.

My mother got her nerve up, strode up to the bar, and managed a few sentences in broken French.

"We're in Belgium," She reported back to me.

"Belgium!" I snorted. Then I smiled, my anger melting away. I was looking at a blackboard with a menu written on it. The room had a cozy and convivial atmosphere and was filled with people eating and drinking. They were serving delicious-smelling food and I was hungry. It really wasn't so bad at all, as it turned out. We had started out early in the morning and had arrived just in time to be served up a hearty midday meal of meat, potatoes, and cabbage followed by black coffee for my mother. We ate the meal, and then Lily bought tickets for a return trip Paris. We took the same train back to Paris we had come in on. It reversed on the tracks and shuttled back to the station.

We took the bullet train from Paris to the Nice, an overnighter, with bunks for us to sleep, but it was a fitful sleep.

***

I opened my eyes and looked at the rocky beach of the Mediterranean, not bothering to lift my head from resting on the window of the bus. I just looked out.

"There's sand on the beaches in some places. Further up, just not here," my mother said.

"There is?"

"Yes."

"And there are no waves!" I said. Then I sat up and turned my head to get a better look. This was almost unacceptable. I watched the movement of the sea, and it just kind of washed up on the shore wave-less, or with what looked like at most, a ripple. Then it sucked itself back out, dragging the little rocks and pebbles.

"It's not an ocean," Lily said. "It's a sea, it's calmer."

"Oh."

There's a unique sound the sea makes on this kind of beach, a sound of washing water and gently clacking rocks. The driver had dropped us off on an empty sidewalk near the port village of Cagnes Sur Mer and I stood listening and became mesmerized. The sound of the lapping and washing and clacking of the rocks and water, and the sea birds, and even sound of an occasional car zooming by merged into absolutely serenity. I felt that I could stay in this moment here forever and be content and never need anything more in this world as I looked down at the smooth rocks that was the beach. I took a deep breath of the fresh salty air and any worries or fatigue I might have felt were forgotten. It felt really good to br there by the beach in the sun; it was something I was familiar with and loved. We were from Southern California.

"It's so beautiful here," I said dreamily.

My mother glanced up from a map she was examining. Behind her, on a hill off in the distance, I saw a walled medieval village abutting up from the flatlands with a turreted castle at the top. Lily shaded her eyes and looked up.

"That must be Haut de Cagnes," she said. "That's where we're going."

In those days, green fields planted with rows of crops lay between the sea and Cagnes, the town at the foot of the hill below Haut de Cagnes. One high-rise poked up on the flatlands between the small fishing port of Cagnes Sur Mer, and the more modern town of Cagnes nestled below the village on the hill. It was twenty kilometers or so down the coast highway from Nice on a bay with Antibes at the far end.

The two of us stared up at the medieval village for moments, disoriented and impressed, just gawking. Then my mother gathered her wits and noticed that the bus stop was across the street. We crossed the street just in time to catch a bus into the center of the Cagnes.

Cagnes was a bustling and modern town, with cafes and shops with plate glass windows lining the streets that displayed delectable-looking edibles and various wares. A throng of teenagers were hanging out and smoking cigarettes by their motor scooters on the main street. I was immediately fascinated by them, and became self-conscious as they watched us walk by. They were beautiful and stylish, and I secretly scrutinized them after they'd lost interest in us and looked away. We were just two tourists. They went back to flirting with one another, cigarettes dangling from lips. They laughed and jostled with each other by their motorbikes on the sidewalk in front of a café where French pop music filtered out onto the street. I lingered a moment and looked inside, spying a young Frenchman in a leather jacket and blue jeans, jamming a pinball machine and then tilting it, and for a moment he glanced sideways at me and our eyes met. He looked away. *He was out of reach,* I thought, *they are out of reach, and they are living in a different world than the world I live in, or ever lived in, but they present an image to aspire to.* I was mulling this over and Lily must have seen the longing on my face.

"They're older than you," my mother softly said. "You're too young for them."

We moved on down the street and came to a narrow steep road that went straight up into Haut de Cagnes. Lily realized we were at the end of the bus line in Cagnes. There was no bus that went up to Haut de Cages because the streets were too narrow.

"We'll have to walk up," Lily said, looking up the hill.

"That's fine with me," I said, smiling. I was in great shape; it was Lily that might have a problem.

We walked slowly up the incline into Haut de Cagnes. The road was straight and narrow, and it was an amazing and beautiful day. Lily seemed to be walking on air after a while, between stopping and catching her breath, that is. I watched my mother's flushed face open up as we climbed the hill. She was entering her own personal kingdom of heaven on earth, and I was witnessing it.

Our first stop was at the bar Tabac, a small establishment three quarters of the way up. It served as the neighborhood café, selling coffee drinks, cigarettes, and alcohol. Out in front, my mother caught her breath from the climb, then launched into a lecture on the nature of French cafés and how superior they were to American bars, how they were inclusive and that I could be a part of the life in this café.

We went in, and once inside I noticed the anticipation ratcheting up on my mother's face. It was as if she knew she was in for something good, but couldn't quite be sure, and it wasn't just because she was attached to her cigarettes and alcohol, necessities of the kind of good life that she wanted. But it was the fact that she didn't yet know that this place, this bar Tabac, was going to be much more than what she had the capacity to imagine it to be. It was all that.

It was a long room filled with small wooden tables and chairs in the back, and bar, cash register, and rack of cigarettes at the front. We sat down in the back at a table.

It was still early in the day, and the café was empty. Lily ordered Anise for herself and a carbonated lemonade drink for me. She gave me a sip of her Anise, a foul-tasting licorice-flavored drink and I gagged at the taste. I went back to my lemonade, concerned a little bit that she was drinking so early in the day, but not too concerned. My mother was an alcoholic, but I was feeling too good right then to worry about it.

"That tastes so awful—"

"You think?"

My mother took another sip, nodded, made a face, then agreed with me. She tried a few more small sips, and she couldn't finish the drink; she left it on the table and we left the café.

On her way out, she purchased a pack of Galois cigarettes, and once we were on the street, she launched into a new monologue on the differences between the French cigarettes, Galois, versus the American cigarettes, Marlboros, and how the French cigarettes were too strong and actually pretty awful but cheaper. She was being thrifty and didn't want to pay the exorbitant price that the Marlboros cost here in France, so should smoke the Galois. We stood in front of the bar Tabac while she unwrapped her newly purchased pack of Galois, and then she lit one up, took a drag, coughed, then tossed it out in disgust on the street. She was obviously rethinking this money-saving strategy and I laughed.

It became evident to me that my mother had found the place she had been looking for on this trip as we walked in Haute de Cagnes. It was written all over her face. It was as if her world was perhaps opening up to an impossibly unimaginably better and wonderful life on every footfall upward into the town. Her face became ever more expectantly radiant, and it was a wonderful thing to behold. She was beautiful, she looked like Grace Kelley, turning 40 and I looked like her, only a younger version. At any rate, my mother couldn't quite trust the feeling she was having, she had to make a connection with Frieda, the name she had been given.

I already knew. I could see it quite plainly that my mother had found what she came here for, and that this town was going to be all she had hoped for and more. We had traveled all this way, and this place was where she wanted to be and where she was meant to be. It was destiny. I was happy to be along. It was my destiny too.

^^^***

At the top of the hill, a group of squat, old women swaddled in black were gathered at a public washroom. They were gossiping and laughing raucously, carrying on in loud voices as they scrubbed clothes at an outdoor fountain in front of the small stone building. They became quiet as we approached and eyed us warily, as if we were an omen of a future that didn't include them. I stared back in curiosity.

"Don't stare," Lily said.

I looked away but watched surreptitiously as the women slapped their washing against the stone basin. They were women from an era that was quickly passing.

They lived through the war, I thought, *encountering American soldiers first and now hordes of American tourists. They lived through World War II.*

"What are those women doing?"

The women commenced back in with their loud gossip.

"They're washer women. They're washing clothes," Lily said.

"They're washing clothes in the middle of town?" My voice had a surprised and slightly imperious tinge to it.

"Yes. They do it here. Not everybody in the world has running water and a washing machine, you know," Lily said impatiently.

"They do it here?"

In reality, my mother was surprised see them as well, and just as curious, and as it turned out, it wasn't too long before they closed the communal washing room for good, within months of our arriving in town. But on that particular day, we walked on up the street past the washerwomen and went into a small grocery store near the plaza at the top of the hill. Lily looked around. It was clear then that everything my mother might need she could get right here in this town and she was satisfied. She was home.

Back outside the store, she looked at me and I could see her mind working, she wanted to know if I felt the same way.

"We'll get in shape walking up and down this hill," she said brightly, her way of saying how she felt about staying.

I didn't respond.

"Do you think you might like to stay here?" She asked.

"You want to stay?" I said.

Lily nodded.

"Okay," I said. It was late fall and I had wanted to go skiing in Switzerland on this European trip, this journey, but I could clearly see it wasn't going to happen. Our trip so far had taken us through London and Paris to the South of France, and it was plain that it was coming to a stop.

"We need to meet Frieda," my mother said.

"Who?"

"Frieda," she said. "Frieda Vorkapitch."

Chapter 4

Frieda was a squat dark woman with an intense demeanor who wore her cropped hair short and dressed in worn corduroys and loose pullover sweaters. When engaged in conversation she would lean forward in her seat and listen with focused concentration, rarely speaking but continually fidgeting with her hands. She would examine and gnaw at her fingers; her nails were chewed to the quick. She was our "person" in Haut de Cagnes, our point of contact, and as such she had no pretense at being anything other than quite useless in the art of human interaction. She barely spoke.

She was a talented sculptress and kept a studio in the village. She was living off inherited wealth, one of the many wealthy women who lived in the general vicinity of Haut de Cagnes, people who had the means to set up a life for themselves up in the South of France. As for Lily and me, this way of life was to be fleeting. Lily was financing our trip by using up the money she had collected from selling her only asset, our house in California.

But back to Frieda. She was a gentle and genial soul, and when she did speak it was softly, and she was obliging and helpful. But, being as she was unable to deliver anything tangible, she brought us to Noel.

Noel. Noel seemed to be at the center of things and was someone who knew a lot of people and talked with many more and they liked her. She was charismatic. She was a negotiator and she was sly; she could be wily and perhaps most importantly in all of this, she spoke fluent French. She would be the person that could help us get situated in Haut de Cagnes. She could help us find a place to live.

Noel was Irish and had the look of the Irish, red hair and pale blue eyes, and was tall and elegant in a streetwise kind of way. She was in her forties, and I thought that at one time in her life she must have been a beauty. She served us tea when we arrived, and we sat in her living room and got acquainted. She immediately took to Lily and me and we to her.

Her house was on the side of Haut de Cagnes that faced the bay, and as the adults talked small talk, I got bored and got up and walked over to the window. I looked out at the sea and a town in the distance.

"That's Antibes," Noel said, pausing in the conversation. She was watching me.

Lily's face went flush with pleasure, "Antibes!" she said breathlessly. She got up and came over and stood with me at the window.

"Do you want to look around?" Noel said.

She took us on a tour of her house. We walked down steep stone steps from the patio outside the main floor of her house to a yard from which the fortress-like wall of the old city dropped away. Then we stood by the wall for moments looking out at over the bay. Underneath her house was an empty apartment full of cobwebs set back and hidden behind vines.

I saw a calculating look develop on my mother's face; she had her eyes on the empty garden apartment, but she was trying to be subtle.

"Is that an apartment?" she asked off-handedly.

"I think it was used as a wine cellar," Noel said.

Lily nodded. "Can I look?" She was already at the door and going inside and I followed her into the dark rooms, cave-like and full of dust and cobwebs.

"This place could be cleaned up," Lily said tentatively.

"It floods in the winter," Noel said. "You can't live here."

Lily nodded, and Noel watched her with a little smile on her face, surprised. She was reading her like a book and Lily blushed and shrugged it off. It was too soon to move in, as much as we needed a place.

Noel led us back upstairs to the main floor, passing through the kitchen and dining area to the living room once again, and then up narrow stairs to her bedroom where she opened the door for us to take a peek. We looked into the tidy spare room with a double bed with a colorful, knitted quilt folded neatly at the foot, and a nightstand covered with bottles of pills. Noel abruptly shut the door. We had been given a calculated glimpse into something private, something Noel had decided to share with us, and I felt a little embarrassed by the intimacy. Noel was sick.

When we sat back down in Noel's living room, Lily was suddenly shy, and Noel quickly stepped in taking the upper hand. She made a call to a real estate agent about finding an apartment, and while speaking on the phone in a loud and slightly imperious voice, in her fluent French, her eyes rested on Lily with an unmistakably hungry and amused look. I noticed it, and so did Frieda, who was slouched on the sofa next to me, watching and fidgeting and chewing her nails. She was fast becoming a footnote. It was obvious that there were sparks flying between Noel and my mother, and Frieda just sat there watching; she and Noel were lovers.

I didn't understand the significance of these things, and I didn't really care, but I noticed Frieda biting her nails nervously and appreciated her nervousness. I smiled at her and Frieda smiled tentatively back.

"Do you play chess?" I said.

"What?" Frieda started and quit biting her hands for a moment. "Yes."

"Do you want to play sometime?"

I could tell Frieda was flattered. She was the type of woman who had very little to do with children, and here I was, a thirteen-year-old girl, wanting to play chess with her. As for me, I was attracted to Frieda's unpretentious awkwardness and her glaring inability to dissemble. I had been ignoring the flirtatious talk going on between Lily and Noel, and Frieda, who had been listening and watching with a guarded expression on her face gave up paying attention as well. It was as if she seemed to acknowledged to herself, "There is nothing I can do if something is going happening between them anyway." Or perhaps she thought, "Noel is sick and this won't go any where anyway." Or maybe she had just been expecting all along for this to happen, that sooner or later Noel would find someone else and was just resigned.

It was just speculation. Frieda agreed to a date, initiated by Noel, to play chess with me the following week, at Noel's house, and Lily would come along as well to supervise. And to visit and get better acquainted.

"Do you play gin rummy?" Frieda said.

I could tell she liked me, and I was open in that way that young people could be, and non-judgmental, and I was friendly. I didn't care about how she dressed, or that she could barely talk. Frieda and I were going to be friends.

"I don't know how to play," I said.

"I can show you," Frieda said." You can play with us at the bar Tabac," she said in her soft voice, then quickly glanced at Lily.

"A bar?" I said. "I can't play in a bar."

Noel and Lily stopped talking and stared at us.

"You can go to the bar Tabac here," Lily said. "We've been there already; I told you it's not like in American bars where you can't go in. It's for everyone."

"Okay . . ." I was unsure, but nodded.

Noel stood up, signaling that the visit was over and Frieda took the cue and quickly jumped up. There would be no delay. As we headed for the door, Noel assured my mother that she would call the real estate agent again on her behalf and set a meeting up, but as for now she had to rest. She had to get back to bed, and suddenly Noel looked frail. Lily frowned and was concerned. Frieda herded us out of the house and into the narrow street in front where she explained things as we walked quickly up toward the plaza.

"What's wrong with her?" I asked.

"She gets tired very easy," Frieda said. "She needs to rest."

"She has cancer," Lily said.

"Is she going to get well?" I said.

"No," Lily said.

Frieda glanced at me with a worried look. We came to a set of wide stone steps set between the old walls that led up the street above, and she bounded up the stairs ahead of us in a determined and energetic fashion. Then she watched and listened to Lily talking to me as she waited at the top.

"It's terminal," Lily said sadly. I saw my mother's face settle in determination. She was going to be involved in this.

"Does that mean she's going to die?" I said.

"Yes." The look of determination was replaced on Lily's face with one of uncertainty.

"It's not going to happen soon," Frieda said as we caught up. "It's years away!"

My mother and I exhaled with relief.

"Years?"

"Yes, a long time."

Chapter 5

The next day, the real estate agent took us to see some available apartments in Haut de Cagnes. The first place she took us was quite impressive. It was spacious and light, and had a dining room furnished with chairs and table and two bedrooms, one for Lily and one for me. It was on the side of a steep hill with a view of Antibes, the same view as Noel's, and had a terraced layout, with rooms on each level and stone steps running the length of it from the bottom to the top.

"This is marvelous!" Lily exclaimed. She sounded giddy.

"I love it," I said, standing in the dining room and gazing at the table. "We can eat breakfast here!"

I imagined enjoying breakfasts of croissants and juice, sitting in this airy space at the table with the sun streaming in.

A gutter ran down the side of the apartment next to a wall on the other side of the steps. The agent, a middle-aged, well-put-together Frenchwoman turned away from my eager face as I talked about breakfast and looked over at the wall and the gutter and frowned.

"How long are you planning on staying?" she said in heavily accented English.

"We're not sure," Lily said. "Why?"

"For the winter?"

"Yes, I think so. We may stay that long"

"Rain runs through here in the winter," she said.

We looked down at the culvert, and it ran the entire length of the apartment from top to bottom.

"I think this used to be a public walkway and they closed it in," the agent explained, moving closer to the steps and examining the culvert.

"Water runs there?" I said, a smile forming on my face.

"Yes," she said. "When it rains it gets to be quite a lot of water going through here. Sometimes it comes up over the steps."

"Like a river?" I said. I was grinning now.

"A creek," the agent said and nodded.

I imagined a rushing creek running through the apartment and looked at the table and chairs.

"But it doesn't reach the table," I said.

"No," the agent said slowly, shaking her head. "It doesn't."

Yes! I could watch the river while eating!

"It's okay with me," I quickly said.

"No," Lily said, shaking her head. "Do you have anything else?"

Yes, she had something else. It was located on a cobblestone alley off the main plaza toward the top of Haut de Cagnes. It had a kitchen and dining area toward the front of the apartment furnished with a dining table and chairs and a single bed used as a couch and living area toward the back. There was another bedroom upstairs and bathroom. It had no view, but it also had no rushing creek running through it. Lily took it immediately, and we moved in the next day. I took the upstairs bedroom and Lily the down-stairs.

That night we went to dinner to celebrate at the one and only restaurant in Haut de Cagnes, run by a young married couple, Marie and Jean.

Jean, a fresh-faced Frenchman, seated us and handed us menus, and Marie poked her head out from the kitchen to see who had arrived. She was a pretty woman with shoulder-length blonde hair who wore just the right amount of black eye-liner and makeup and skirts of modest length, carefully thought out, to her knees. We caught a glimpse of only her head when she looked out; Marie quickly withdrew back into the kitchen. As it turned out, she always did this. She always had to know who was in the restaurant at any given time and was somewhat furtive in her surveillance techniques. I noticed Jean glance at her with an unmistakably weary expression, as Marie disappeared behind the door to the kitchen, and then his face went blank as he turned back to manning the small bar.

Lily ordered snails. Snails!

I ordered *poulet* and potatoes, and they were like nothing I had ever seen or tasted before. Marie was an excellent cook, and the potatoes tasted better at that moment as I ate them than anything I had ever tasted. They were nothing like any potato that I had ever tasted in my life up to that point. I offered one up to my mother.

"Yes," Her eyes literally glittered as she chewed the potato with pleasure. "I wonder how she made those." They were round and somewhat crispy and soft inside.

Lily offered up a snail and I ate it, rolling it around on my tongue and savoring the buttery garlic flavor, and then I bit into it. The consistency was chewy and rubbery, and I just about gagged. I didn't spit it out and managed to swallow but made a face and Lily laughed.

"You don't like them?"

"No!"

It took a minute and then I said, "Do you?"

"Yes," Lily said definitively, looking down at her plate. "You just don't have a sophisticated palate."

"They're too chewy, yuck . . ."

"They are bit rubbery," she concurred. "You're right. Maybe not the best snails I've eaten." Then she ate the whole plateful as I watched, as if she was trying to make a point.

Marie came out of the kitchen after we finished our meal and introduced herself. She exuded a friendly warmth, but I could tell she was unhappy. She moved her body in stiff mechanical movements. I thought she might be the type of person who thought she had been destined for better things in life and was now settling for less; and that might have been true, but as it turned out her marriage with Jean was falling apart and this was the source of her unhappiness. Perhaps both of these things were true, or I was rushing to judgment, but we didn't find these things out that first night we ate in her restaurant. We saw only a woman who presented herself as a proper French wife exuding an undercurrent of discontent. It was a discontent I recognized, something common among women in those days and generally ignored, something I was keenly and uncomfortably aware of but didn't understand.

At any rate, Marie sat down with us and welcomed us to Haut de Cagnes after Lily told her we had just moved there, and pointed to Jean at the bar and told us that he was her husband and I was quiet. I could see my mother feeling suddenly awkward and self-conscious in the conversation, speaking her bad French, and I watched silently as the two adults negotiated communicating in stilted phrases back and forth until at last, finally, Marie got up and went back to the kitchen. I relaxed and Lily ordered espresso coffee.

I watched Lily pour two teaspoons of sugar in the espresso, then sip the small cup of dark liquid. She looked very happy. It was obvious that she loved this place.

Chapter 6

Christopher had strait, brown, lanky hair with a forelock that fell across the top of his forehead and deep-set blue-green eyes. He was intelligent and troubled, and sometimes calculating. He was thirteen, the same age as me, and wearing short pants. He quickly explained why he would be leaving the short pants behind shortly, as soon as he turned fourteen, which would be very soon, a rite of passage not to be dwelt on, and sure enough I never saw him in short pants again after that first night.

We had been living in our apartment for only a couple of days when he appeared. It was nightfall, and he was standing at the end of our alley with a group of boys. They were talking in loud animated French, and I didn't know it, but they were discussing the arrival of Lily and myself in Haut de Cagnes.

Lily and I had just finished dinner and could hear them from inside the apartment.

"What's that noise?" Lily said.

"Someone's talking out there."

"They're so loud."

Lily opened the door and poked her head out to take a look. The boys ducked out of sight around the corner, and she came back inside. It was quiet for a few minutes. Then they started up again.

"They're back," I said.

"You look," Lily said impatiently. "I didn't see anything."

I stepped out the front door and looked up the alley. I saw them and stood there listening to the rise and fall of their voices, not understanding what they were saying. They looked back down the alley at me. Our apartment was at the end where the narrow street took a sharp turn.

"Alloo!" a boy called out

"Hello," I said.

"American!" someone shouted and a loud discussion followed. Then one of them pushed Christopher forward out of the group. He stumbled, and then seeing me watching him, straightened up and walked down the alley toward me in a determined and stilted gate.

"Are you American?" he said in an upper class clipped British accent.

"Yes, you're English?"

"Yes."

"Do you speak French?" he said, glancing back at the group of boys.

"No. What are they saying?"

The French boys were watching and muttering among themselves. Christopher looked back again at them.

"They're talking about you," he said.

"They are?"

"Yes." He nodded. He was smiling now.

"What are they saying?"

Christopher turned and faced me. "They think you are very beautiful. They wanted to know if you are American."

"Oh, I see." I was embarrassed by his directness, but I liked it. I smiled at him and he extended out his hand to me.

"I'm Christopher."

"I'm Suzanne."

There was a burst of laughter and loud chatter from the end of the alley right after we shook hands. I looked up and saw one of them mime the handshake. Christopher scowled.

"What are they saying now?"

Christopher yelled out something in French to them and gestured for them to go away. They ducked out of sight behind the wall and it was quiet.

"They're jealous because I'm talking to you," he said. "They don't speak English."

The determining factor in this matter, as to which boy would have the chance to be with me, was that it was going to be the one who spoke

English. Boys could be practical about these things, without question.

"Do you want to walk up to the plaza?" Christopher said. He sounded distracted and was still staring up the alley into the darkness.

"What are you looking at?" I said.

"I don't know if they're still up there," he said. "They could be right around the corner."

"Oh." I looked for them. "I don't see them."

Christopher put his index finger to his lips. "Shhhhh," he said. Then he cocked his head and listened. "I think it's okay, let's go." He started to walk away.

"I have to ask my mother!"

He stopped and took a quick look around and then at the door to our apartment. It was ajar.

"Okay, go ask your mother," he quickly said.

"Do you want to meet her?"

"I'll meet her next time, is that all right?" he said.

I slowly nodded. "I think so."

I went inside the apartment and a moment later Lily poked her head out. She could see his shadowy figure waiting halfway up the alley. Christopher was standing and leaning against the wall in a moon shadow having moved away from the door. He looked back her silently.

"Is that him?" she said. "Why doesn't he come over and say hello?"

"His name is Christopher. He wants to meet you, but next time, okay?"

Lily understood. She nodded. "Okay," she said. "Come back an hour. And tell Christopher I want to meet him."

We walked to the end of the alley and Christopher peeked around the corner apprehensively. "They're gone," he said with relief.

"Aren't they your friends?"

"Yes, they're my friends, but I'm glad they're gone."

He relaxed now and was full of confidence as we strolled toward the plaza at the top of the hill. At the far end of the plaza, opposite the church, was a thick low wall and we stopped there. Behind the town were open green gardens of flowers and paths that led into woods and far off in the distance the town of Vence. We stood and looked out at the dark shapes of hills and at the twinkling lights of Vence under a clear, black, starry sky.

Christopher told me he lived with his grandparents in a house on the other side of Haut de Cagnes and that they had moved to Vence to retire there.

"And you?" he said.

"I'm here with my mother," I said, then asked him about his parents and there was a moment of awkwardness.

His parents weren't around, he said, sounding suddenly remote. "I live with my grandparents."

"I live with my mother, she's divorced. She divorced my father and we came here" I said.

"Your mother is divorced?" Christopher said.

"Yes."

He was quiet for a moment. Then he said, "My mother left my father. She went off with another man."

"She did?"

Christopher nodded and was silent for moments and then he said solemnly. "She shouldn't have done it."

I didn't say anything, and then I said, "What's she like?"

"My mother is very beautiful," he said, and then he looked directly at me. He had a way of doing this that was disarming and all encompassing, he had a laser-like focus. "Like your mother. Your mother is very beautiful."

"You think she's beautiful?" I said. I didn't think of my mother in this way. She was, well, she was just Lily, my mother.

"Yes, she is."

This boy was different from the boys in California, I thought. They wouldn't talk this way back home, about his mother and my mother being very beautiful.

"People should stay together if they get married," Christopher said.

"They fall out of love."

He shook his head. "They shouldn't get married in the first place then, not if they are going to just *fall out of love*."

I thought about what he said, about the truth of it, that it was so absolutely true.

I noticed a light, flowery fragrance in the air. "What's that smell? It smells really good here," I said.

"It's the flowers," Christopher said shortly.

"What flowers?"

"They grow flowers behind the town on the hills. You haven't been back there?'

I shook my head, no.

"I'll take you there," he said enthusiastically. "I'll take you to the woods, I know a really good place"

I nodded absently.

"You want to come, don't you?"

"Yes."

"And I'll show you where I live also, you can meet my grandmother."

"Okay."

There was something in my voice, or on my face, that Christopher saw and he wasn't sure what it was, so he turned away from me abruptly. I didn't sound enthusiastic. What was it? Disinterest? It wasn't disinterest at all, but the nature of the conversation itself. I just didn't know what to feel talking about these things and took the easy way out, the standoffish way out.

"We should go back," he said. "It's been an hour. I don't want your mother to get mad."

"Okay." I was surprised; it had barely been an hour.

We walked back across the plaza, talking about other things, unimportant things, and about Christopher's favorite place in the woods, the place that he would take me to.

A few days later, someone knocked on our door, and Lily opened it to find Christopher standing on the steps. She looked down at him and listened sympathetically as he nervously stuttered through an introduction with a flushed face. Then she asked him if he'd like to come in.

"Oh, we'll just leave now, if you don't mind," he said breezily. We were going to go for a walk, and he was going to show me his house and some books to lend me, and, yes, his grandmother would be there at his house, he said.

"I can share my books with Suzanne" he explained, as if something needed explaining. "English books," he elaborated.

My mother smiled her approval. It was obvious that she liked him, and I knew he didn't need to be worried. I knew it was because she was sold completely on his British accent.

"And then we are going for a walk in the woods," I added just as Christopher had his hand on the door and was edging out.

"What woods?" Lily said.

"There are woods behind the town. We're just going for a short walk," Christopher quickly said and turned and stopped. Lily scrutinized him closely as he squirmed. His already rosy cheeks turned redder.

"All right," she finally said.

"You shouldn't have said anything about the woods," Christopher said after we left.

"Why not?"

"Your mother didn't like it."

"She said it was okay."

"She didn't like it," he said. "And bedsides, it's a secret place, I don't want any grownups to know about it."

We walked along the road toward his house on the side of the village facing Nice, with buildings and houses on one side and a fortress wall built into the cliff on the other side dropping down. Below, and in the distance, was a lush valley that ran down into the open fields near Cagnes Sur Mer, dotted with scattered farms and country houses. A river ran through the middle of the valley and a road ran along both sides of the river. I looked down admiring the view, struck by the beauty.

"Do you like Charles Dickens?" Christopher said, wanting my attention. The view was nothing much to him; he'd walked this road countless times.

"Yes! *Oliver Twist* is one of my favorite books."

"*Oliver Twist*? Yes, I like that one, but I prefer *David Copperfield*," he said. I looked away from the view and at him. He sounded prissy, maybe it was the accent.

"Is it? I haven't read it."

"Oh, yes," he said with certainty, cocking his head slightly back and sideways. "It's the better book of the two books. I'll lend it to you if you like."

We stopped at his house for a short visit and he introduced me to his grandmother. His grandfather was out of sight. As it turned out, he was perpetually out of sight for a reason that I never knew. I never met him.

Christopher's grandmother peered down at me with a look of slight distaste on her face, as if she was examining a dead fish. This was a look I had encountered before, the kind of look some adults gave children when the truth of the matter was that they really didn't like children at all and could just as well do without them.

She was dressed in a gray-flowered dress that fell below her knees, an old lady dress, and wearing a pair of glasses perched a reddish, bulbous nose. She was a proper English matron, formal, unsmiling, and cold. I wanted to get away from her. When we finally left, the old lady squeezed out a tight smile, relieved to see us leave the house.

We walked into the woods at the rear of the village and made our way down a slope through the trees. Enthused, Christopher forged ahead.

"What do you think?" he yelled, twigs snapping underneath as we walked. He was excited.

I stopped and looked around. Pine needles lay scattered on the floor of the woods like a carpet, making it easy to walk, and the trees were evenly spaced apart in an almost geometrical fashion. I'd never seen anything like it. I had just come from Malibu Canyon, where I'd crawled through heavy underbrush sometimes, we called it "bush whacking," my best friend Terry and I, when hiking back home in the Santa Monica Mountains.

"It's easy to walk here." I said. I started walking again.

"Is it? What do you mean?"

"I mean, it's easy to walk through here," I said. "It isn't wild."

Christopher stopped and turned around. "What do you mean it isn't wild?" he said.

"It doesn't seem wild," I said. "That's all."

It wasn't wild. A hundred or thousand souls had trampled these woods and reseeded and re-planted the trees.

"It's not like the woods in America," I continued on. "It's so wild there that it's difficult to walk at all in the woods, sometimes—"

Christopher stopped in a small clearing, his favorite spot, and sat down. He looked deflated. "You don't like it?" he said. I already recognized a certain timbre in his voice. It had a peevish-sounding quality, higher than how he usually spoke, and his British accent was more pronounced.

"I didn't say that. I like it," I replied.

He pulled a thistle from the ground. "But it isn't like America. Where it's wild," he said in a sarcastic tone.

"Yeah," I said.

He was quiet a moment and then said, "I shouldn't have brought you here."

"Christopher! I like it here." I could see that he was bothered, and his favorite place had been sullied. I had sullied it somehow, sullied some idea of his that he had about this place.

"Okay," he said and then he looked around. "You're right. It isn't wild."

At that moment a squat, bent, old woman dressed in a black sack-like dress and draped in a shawl appeared in the distance, shuffling through the trees. She had a huge bundle of faggots on her back. She was collecting wood, stooping and bending, reaching to pick the sticks up off the forest floor.

"Look at that!" I said. "Look at that woman, what is she doing?"

"She's gathering wood," Christopher said and looked sideways at me as if I was an idiot.

"That's why it's so easy to walk here. They pick up the all the sticks off the ground!"

Christopher didn't say anything. We watched the old woman, the only sound was her shuffling movements and snapping branches.

"You would never see something like that in America," I said.

"You wouldn't?" he said, sounding utterly dispirited.

"No."

"I've never seen her here before or anyone like her," he said definitively.

"You haven't?"

He shook his head. "No."

After a moment, he said, "This place isn't secret at all. A million people walk through here." He smirked and I grinned, and he looked at me with an incredulous look, like "Can you believe it?"

He stood up. "Let's go." This place had no magic.

Chapter 7

Just as she welcomed us into her home on that first day that Frieda brought us to her house, Noel welcomed us into her life. Lily and I became part of a group, Noel's group. Frieda and Marion, a friend of Noel's who took care of her were closest to Noel, but my mother soon eclipsed Frieda's place in the circle. Marion played an entirely different role, a role my mother would never take on. She was the nursemaid, on call and lurking on the periphery of things, or so it seemed to me, keeping a keen eye out for Noel. She was a quiet woman and rarely spoke unless spoken to, with a timid and serious demeanor with an exceptional ability for making herself invisible. I found out later that she had been in the camps as a young girl when she was my age. She was a concentration camp survivor. She had lost her entire family in the camps.

Marion disapproved of Lily right away, and after a brief attempt at genteelness was quite open about her feelings. Perhaps it was jealousy, or perhaps it was something else, that she sensed something about Lily, that my mother was not the person who would go the distance with Noel, something she herself was prepared to do. And as for me? She was grudgingly polite. Perhaps it was that my blonde hair and blue eyes, my Aryan looks were an unhappy reminder of her own life as a young Jew who ended up in a concentration camp at my age. I didn't understand any of this. I saw a woman who barely tried to conceal a scowl, a woman with uncertain eyes who made me uneasy. There was something in her eyes that I saw when she looked at me, and it was something I was unfamiliar with, an incredulity and a yearning for recognition that she was there, and that something had happened, and I should know about it. She had been was in the holocaust. But I was a thirteen year old from California and didn't know and didn't understand.

At any rate, Noel's circle of friends also included Ken, an aging queen who sported turtlenecks and scarves, a homosexual (was what he called himself), who checked in on Noel and cooked her meals from time to time. He was uncomfortable relating to a teenage girl. This little group had organized itself into a schedule of caring for Noel. And then we arrived.

It must have been like a breath of fresh air for Noel. Lily came into Noel's life not as a person to be a caretaker, not to nurse her in her sickness or help her in her dying, but as a lover. As such, she was an interloper and disrupted the schedule and order of things. Lily came as a lover in this world, in this life, and she must have been a reminder that things were not over for Noel, not just yet. Marion was polite at first but soon became openly resentful when she saw that we were staying. Ken stayed away. Frieda understood. I didn't know that Noel would fall in love with my mother, or that they would become lovers at the time, and I didn't care about it either. There had been enough time from my parents' divorce, and I guess there was enough distance. I knew that I liked Noel.

It is only some times in life when people come together, in a special place and time, like points of tiny light creating an ever wider circle, like individual dancing atoms of energy moving around one another and creating something even bigger and alive. It's something we can't control, and when it comes, when the opportunity to be part of it presents itself a person must be ready and willing to join in because it is a matter of timing.

That was such a time and place for my mother and myself in Haut de Cagnes, and for me, it was my first time to be a part of such a thing. My mother didn't hesitate, and I followed her and we became part of something bigger than ourselves, part of a community.

We became part of a group, an expansive and elastic group, which included other characters in the village, many of whom were lesbians and/or artists and who lived in the village itself or the surrounding environs. I could tell it was deeply gratifying for my mother to be part of this and it was giving her a once-in-a-lifetime happiness, fleeting perhaps, but the kind of happiness that sometimes just fell into a person's lap when you were in the right place at the right time. I watched my mother blossom and I thought that she must have been lonely for years, it was gratifying for me to see her happiness.

Chapter 8

Yes, we were part of something bigger than ourselves, my mother and I, and a certain individual named Pat, who was sitting in our new apartment on Rue d'Or, was also a part of it. Pat was visiting with my mother when I came in from outside (I'd been exploring the village), and the two of them sounded as if they had known one another for years by the way they were carrying on. They were both a little drunk.

Pat was a fortyish attractive French lesbian with a puffy, tanned face. She wore light makeup and tight clothes, and usually had a colorful silk scarf tucked in at her neck. Her gray hair was cut stylishly short.

She was short and had a kind of pixyish quality, emoting a warmth and boozy charm, speaking English with a smarmy terrible accent. She had a glass of wine in front of her and a cigarette in her hand, and when she spoke it was difficult for me to tell if she was lisping from drinking or if it was just her bad English. It didn't matter. She was one of those adults who found it natural and easy to banter with children, and after a few moments I knew that I liked her.

She had a lover, Mericke, who wasn't with her that night, and who in my estimation upon acquaintance was quite the opposite in the charm department. Mericke was a tall, elegant woman from an upper class French family with a severe demeanor and stiff upright posture, who always seemed to either scowl or look down her nose at me in disapproval when we encountered one another, as if she was questioning the right to my very existence in the universe itself. As it turned out, she vastly disapproved of me being a present in any fashion among this group, thinking it a bad idea and that perhaps they were a bad influence. When around Mericke, the best that I could hope for was to be ignored.

The two of them, Pat and Merrick, lived together in a high rise on the flats below Haut de Cagnes, the new lone structure that jutted up incongruously amidst the vegetable plots. During those years, the French were smitten by these modern buildings; they had the conveniences Americans took for granted.

It was early evening, and my mother and Pat were sitting and talking and smoking and drinking. I got bored. I sat on the couch, yards away from where they were sitting at the table, listening to Pat's melodic, husky voice rise and fall, not quite deciphering everything she was saying in her thick accent and glad that I wasn't expected to respond. Then I heard the signal. It was a low whistling sound.

Pat and Lily stopped talking.

"What's that noise?" Pat said.

I got up from the couch and went over to the front door. I stood by the door listening and the three of us were silent. We heard it again, a soft rising sharp whistle, which then fell away. Christopher had just learned this new skill, whistling through his teeth and was keen to put it to use.

"It's Christopher," I said.

Christopher wanted as little to do with adults as possible, including my mother, and had devised a method of meeting with me without interception. He'd whistle his low shrill whistle as a signal, and I'd come out and we would meet in the plaza.

"Christopher?" Pat said.

I nodded.

"A boy?"

"Yes. He's whistling for me."

"Like a dog?"

"No. No," I said impatiently. "Not like a dog. It's a signal."

Pat went to the door and poked her head out. Then she came back in. "I see him over there. Why doesn't he come and knock on the door?"

"It's a signal for me," I said. "Like a secret signal."

"I see." Pat smiled; she was high. She would be smiling high or not. "A signal." She sat back down. "She has a boyfriend," she said to Lily.

"He doesn't want to come to the door and talk to me," Lily said and they both snickered.

"That makes sense. He's a smart boy," Pat said.

Lily laughed, "He's a nice boy."

"Who whistles for you like a dog?" Pat said.

I shrugged. Pat just didn't understand and was ready to think the worst because he was a boy, I was thinking. She doesn't like boys, I was thinking.

"Can I go?" I said.

"Come back in an hour."

"Have fun," Pat said and raised her glass in a toast. "To love!" She elaborated with a smarmy smile. I giggled and slid out the door. Christopher was waiting halfway up the alley.

"Good! You came. I thought you weren't going to come." He was excited.

"I told you I'd come."

He was going to teach me how to French kiss on this special occasion and had the place and the route carefully planned in advance as to where the kiss would take place. We started out, walking briskly along in the dark. I felt nervous and also excited. Being with Christopher, and having the opportunity to French kiss was an adventure! The world was my oyster.

"Have you done it?" he said.

"What?"

"Kissed!"

"Just with my mouth closed." It had been at Disney Land, at my middle school graduation outing with a boy who rubbed his lips against mine as we rode into a darkened tunnel on a ride. I thought of that boy, how utterly bland he had been. Nice, but boring. Our relationship, if you could call it that, was an imitation of what we thought how a boy and girl should be.

Christopher put his lips against the back of his hand and dryly smooched it. "That's nothing," he said. "It doesn't count. It's like doing that, kissing the back of your hand."

I nodded. Clearly he was a man of experience.

We walked off the main plaza, down some steps to Noel's street, and went under a house in an open garage to an overlook where we could see out over the bay, standing in the shadows, looking out at the lights of Antibes twinkling in the distance, Christopher kissed me. He kissed me with his mouth open, his tongue seeking, a wide-open, searching, probing kiss.

"Did you like it?" he said after, his face searching.

"Yeah." I wasn't quite sure that I liked it. It was squishy.

I liked it enough that we did it again. We were quiet for a few moments, then we walked back to the plaza. Our world was full of kisses after that first kiss. Big, wet-tongue kisses.

Chapter 9

We were visiting Noel and with her typical flourish she suggested we all go—Lily, myself, and Frieda—to the bar Tabac. Frieda could make good and teach me how to play gin rummy, Noel said, with a sharp eye on Frieda, who immediately sat upright at attention, and Noel could introduce Lily around.

It was crowded when we got there, as it usually was most every night. A slender dark man sitting with an older gray-haired woman waved us to the back to a table. Noel introduced us to Kathleen and Lando. Kathleen was one of the many expats who lived in the village. She was a "lady" and a distinguished and vibrant personage, who had at one time been a concert pianist and another time a cabaret performer over the course of her life. She lived down the street from Noel and gave piano lessons. She and my mother took to one another, immediately becoming fast friends, and from then on, after that initial meeting, the two of them always seemed to have endless topics of interest to discuss together in high-pitched, excited voices. And then there was Lando. Sweet Lando.

Lando was a young man in his thirties from Brooklyn, with soulful, brown eyes and a thick, well-groomed, curly, black beard. He was veteran of the Korean War living on a disability pension and had decided to become a painter. He was living out a dream; the life of the *artiste* in Southern France. He wasn't any good it quickly became known to us, but no one had the heart to tell him. He worked diligently at his craft producing canvas after canvas of small oil paintings of Haut de Cagnes. "Cezanne knock offs," Noel said dismissively that very night, with him sitting right there. Lando said nothing and just smiled enigmatically.

We set about playing cards. A foursome started in on a game of gin rummy, Kathleen, Lando, Frieda, and myself. Noel, quite the social butterfly, talked and laughed with any and all of the people in the vicinity of our table or passing by. She introduced Lily to everyone she knew. It was grand!

Frieda kept her head down and concentrated on explaining the rules of the game to me. I felt shy and said hello softly when introduced to the grownups. I was happy to be included and to play cards at the bar Tabac. And as for the adults, they seemed happy to have a young girl among them. I was turning heads.

"You would make a great model," Lando said. "Can I paint you?"

Lily quickly focused her attention on Lando with laser eyes. "Where?" she said in a soft, short, and suspicious tone, trying not to draw attention to herself. She didn't wasn't to spoil the overall convivial mood.

"Hmmm," Lando said and stroked his beard. A small smile played across his lips and he looked at Lily. "There's a lot of good places," he said. "The woods behind the town. Or in the flower fields. Yes, the flower fields behind the town. That would make a good backdrop." He nodded, as if the nodding would explain something that needed to be explained, that his motivation was innocent. Then he leaned back and took a long look at me, striking a pose as if he was visualizing a painting and waited for an answer.

I looked at my mother, who was now tight-lipped and silent, her face a closed mask.

"I think it would be all right," I said tentatively. "Is it okay—"

"We'll see," Lily interjected in a tone that said no. "I'll let you know."

Lily was suspicious of Lando and only grudgingly friendly. She had yet to find out what kind of person he was, that he was a warm and trustworthy man and a loyal friend to Noel.

Noel watched Lily with a blank expression on her face as this exchange unfolded, and Lando glanced at her briefly, maybe hoping Noel would intercede on behalf of him and his character. She was silent and impassive; she was drooping now and had no energy for this, her sickness all around the edges of her. Lando scrutinized her and sucked a last drag from his cigarette, then stubbed it out.

We played cards.

"Gin!" I laid down my hand with a flourish and grinned, but it was an empty gesture. I didn't know the game yet and hadn't really won.

"What?" Frieda looked up. I showed her my hand, and Frieda shook her head no and smiled her typical tiny smile.

"You didn't win," she said and went back to her hand.

The place was humming with activity, with people laughing and talking, smoking and drinking.

"Gin!" Kathleen said, and she laid her cards down with an even bigger flourish.

She was the winner, and Lily and I soon found out that she was undisputedly the best player of gin rummy among them. Kathleen, in her flowing skirts and fine leather boots, in her fitted jackets and silk scarves, always made-up and carefully groomed, the lady was a shameless card shark.

She gathered up the small pot of money from the center of the table and started talking about the piano with Lily. She was trying to drum up business and she wanted me to take lessons. Lily politely listened, then quietly assured her she would ask later if I would take piano lessons from her, which she knew I would decline. I hated the piano, and the idea of piano lessons, having had an unfortunate experience with a piano teacher at age five. My mother had brought in a sour old lady to give me lessons, and I remember the "No!" said in a severe and weary voice. The teacher stopped me midway through a drill. I had failed and I remember the smell of her bad breath as she looked down at me pityingly "You didn't practice, did you?"

Noel was distinctly pale.

Lando stood up. "Let me take you home," he said.

"We should go," Lily said.

"Stay. Stay," Noel said with a weak smile, waving a hand. She was fading fast.

"I'll walk you home," Lando said.

He stood up and made a path for Noel and escorted her through the crowd toward the front of the bar. Lily watched them as they left, and I wondered about him and his relationship with Noel. Lando cared for Noel. They loved one another. Lando loved and admired Noel in a worshipful way, and Noel loved Lando like an older sister loves a little brother.

"Another game?" Kathleen said, paying Lando and Noel no mind whatsoever other than to wave a curt goodbye. She was all business and gin rummy. So we stayed and played another round for another small sum of money, Lily playing in the next round taking Lando's seat. Kathleen won.

Chapter 10

I got a bike and I started riding horses. I got the bike first and rode it continually in the plaza area by the wall opposite the church. This area was paved and flat with a section of gravel, as opposed to cobblestones that covered the rest of the plaza.

Back and forth in lazy, crazy-eight loops I'd ride, thinking about home and thinking about my brother John, and my father, going up and over the dips and bouncing up off a small gulley into the air in a small jump. There was a feeling that had crept in and lodged in me, a feeling that had stayed with me since my experience in the bed and breakfast in London, when I lay in bed afraid and my mother was out drinking. I didn't want to acknowledge it, but it was there like an infection eating away at me, like a sickness inside that taken up permanent residence and it made me feel apart. My mother had asked both of us if we wanted to go to Europe and Jon had declined, while I had said yes. And when I asked why he wasn't coming, she had shrugged and said that he didn't want to come, that he wanted to stay home and in school with his friends, with my father. My brother was back in California with my father and I was here with my mother, and we were a thousand miles apart.

On our flight over, laying across an empty row of seats at the front and listening to the roar of the London-bound jet, an old-fashioned, noisy propjet, I had felt incredibly happy to be up in the air and flying across the ocean through the night. I thought about John and him not being there, regretting that he was missing this and knowing in my heart I had made the right choice to come. I thought maybe he was a member of that group of people who preferred to stay in a small, familiar world rather than experience something new and bigger, something unknown, and I wondered if it was fear and then differences between us had seemed suddenly very wide, like a thousand miles apart and now we really were... I missed him and wished he was with us and then something in me died and then the feeling went away.

A stewardess had walked by and smiled down at me. She was dressed in a dark blue uniform, a short skirt, jacket, and a cap, and then she bent down solicitously to me as she gave me a blanket. I covered my bare legs and pulled the blanket up over my dress to my shoulders, then nestled my head into the pillow. People dressed up to fly in those days, and stewardesses wore sexy uniforms. I was wearing a dress and nylons. The sixties were about to explode, and John just wanted to surf—the water, the ocean, and the yin and yang of it was something I would never understand. What I cared about was the Beatles. The Beatles had come to America, and the world was full of promise and new beginnings ,and I was on my way to London! Thoughts of John had slipped away into a deep recess in my mind.

Thinking about my brother made only made me feel worse. It seemed like our differences were an unbridgeable gulf we were so completely different. I didn't think of anything at all. I just rode my bike.

The spot was a perfect spot for bike riding with a small culvert to dip down and rise through and then bounce out of, good for a variety of skids, to be performed carefully so as not to fall, and smooth pavement, something that there was a not a surfeit of in the village. Pulling up on the handle bars on my bike, fenders and scrapes and all, I rode back and forth in loops and dips and jumps.

People who worked in the plaza soon noticed me. I was hard to miss—the blonde American girl looping absently around on her bike. I became a familiar figure. Christopher, passing through on the periphery of the plaza on his expensive racing bike, stopped and watched.

Next door to the church was a nightclub, a cabaret with walls that were covered with art work, pencil drawings of famous and not-so-famous people who had passed through and attended the shows. Suzy Solidor, an aging cabaret singer, was there. I paused and looked over at her; she looked strange to me, heavily made up, and dressed in a long, tight dress and with a fox fur draped around her neck. She looked back at me as I sat on my bike across the square. She was standing in front of the door to her club. I was resting with one leg against the low wall, propping me up on as I sat on the bike, and we both looked away, me at Vence off in the distance. I turned back and watched her go through the small black door in the wall under a sign that read "Suzy Solidor." I thought about my father and I saw his face in my mind and my lonely feeling came back. We had started to drift apart before I left with my mother for Europe, it had happened after he had moved out. I only saw him on the weekends after that now he was a continent away.

"It's almost more fun having a bike like yours. I wish I had your bike," Christopher said. He had whistled for me at sunset, and we were walking in the plaza.

"But yours is nicer!" I said, surprised.

"Yours is better for riding here in the town. I have to be so careful. Mine's too nice and I can only ride it on smooth pavement."

"Oh." I nodded.

"I used to have one like yours and my grandmother bought me this new one."

"That was nice of her."

"I liked the old one better, but I can't say anything about it because she bought me this new one."

I laughed, but I felt sorry for him, what with his grandmother trying to please him and so absolutely missing the mark. There was trouble for him, between him and his grandmother.

"Do you like living with her?"

"Yes." Christopher nodded, but his eyes took on a familiar glazed look. We were silent for a moment, with things left unsaid.

"Do you miss your father?" he said.

"Yes," I said. "Your grandmother wasn't very friendly to me. I don't think she liked me."

"She liked you, she's just like that, that's just how she is," Christopher said, sounding insistent. He was bothered.

"Okay."

"You should come and meet her again, she likes you. I'll ask her to have you over for tea."

"Tea? You want me to come over for tea?" The timbre of my voice was higher than usual and sounded squeaky. I couldn't believe he was asking me over for *tea*

He looked earnest and nodded. "Yes, we'll have tea and something to eat—"

"Will we have cookies with the tea?"

He frowned. "We could have cookies, I suppose."

"Cookies and tea?" I giggled. "So when? What time do we have the tea? Like at high noon?"

He didn't see what was funny and his mood changed. "In the afternoon!" He was annoyed.

"Okay, okay. It's just that we never have *tea* in California."

"Well, you're not in California now are you? You're here. We have tea here!" His face was flushed.

"Okay, I'll come for tea."

"Good. It's settled then. I'll ask my grandmother."

Chapter 11

Noel had been a horsewoman in her youth and used to go fox hunting.

Fox hunting! Now, I was a girl who was in love with horses. I had of course seen photographs and read about fox hunting in books, and it seemed like something that would be very desirable and exciting to do, and romantic beyond the pale of a doubt, but I hadn't thought about the part where they actually killed the fox.

"I want to go fox hunting!" I said.

"And kill the fox?" Noel said.

I frowned. I had only imagined the part where they ran across green fields and jumped fences. "Do they kill it?"

Noel nodded enthusiastically. "Mhmmm."

"They do? How?"

"The hounds flush it out," she said. She explained the part where they trap the fox, and it could be quite gory, she elaborated, what with the hounds attacking and ripping it to shreds.

"Uh huh." I felt a little sick.

"But sometimes they let it go," she continued. "Sometimes they call off the hounds when it hides. But not usually." Noel scrutinized me, looking pleased with herself.

"Where does it hide?" I said.

"It hides in a warren."

"A warren?"

"Yes, a foxhole in a thicket. The hounds surround it, howling and snarling and barking."

"No!"

Noel smiled and nodded. "They do."

"But it's fun to chase it, jumping over fences and galloping across fields?" I asked.

"Yes," she said.

"I wouldn't want to kill the fox," I said, "but I want to go fox hunting."

Lily was listening and looked thoughtful. Perhaps she was thinking about Noel on a hunt, in riding gear, and seated on a large, brown jumper in the midst of a group of horses, lively well-bred steeds, thoroughbreds chomping at the bit and ready to go. Noel, dressed in jodhpurs and a tailored, red jacket, wearing long leather boots and a black cap on her head, her horse jostling in the middle of the group. They were preparing for the hunt, waiting for the signal to start the run across the English countryside and jumping stone fences. What a sight! This was what I saw in my mind, not a dead fox. I was sold on Noel.

Not too long after this conversation, it was decided that I would start riding, and take jumping lessons. Noel knew a couple in the village, two women, one of whom had a teenage daughter, and one who rode with her daughter at a nearby riding academy. They could kill two birds with one stone—introduce me to a potential friend (the daughter), and sign me up at the riding stable.

Kathryn was barely friendly when we met. She was a fortyish French woman who had left a marriage and taken up with a woman named ZaZou. ZaZou, who I thought cut quite a dashing figure wore her jet-black hair in the style of a flouncy pompadour set off by her smoky gray eyes, and dressed in black, including a three-quarter-length black leather jacket over tailored silk shirts.

As for Kathryn, she was thoroughly middle class, and the bourgeoisie of France I discerned, possess a suffocating pretension that far surpassed their brethren of the American middle class and as such could seem to literally suck the air out of the space that they occupied. I experienced this effect most of time when in the presence of Kathryn, my breathing seemingly reduced to the absolute minimal amount of air intake needed for sustenance. I made every effort to not make a sound when with Kathryn so as not to attract undo attention to myself and found it difficult to even look at her mask-like face.

I could never quite put my finger on why I had this extreme reaction to her, especially since I found her partner, ZaZou, to be an intriguing figure, what with the black leather jacket and Elvis haircut. At any rate, all that came later, and in time, the feeling about Kathryn dissipated.

On our first visit to the stable, Noel drove Lily and me out to the "academy" as she called it in her car where we would meet up with Kathryn and Anik, the teenage daughter. Kathryn was going to introduce us to the riding master.

Noel owned a green Mercedes Benz, which she kept parked at a remote location, and the three of us breezed down the highway along the sea toward Nice, enjoying the ride and then turned inland.

The stable was located in the countryside and surrounded by fields of vegetables and hedgerows, and small clumps and thickets of woods. Stone farmhouses dotted the landscape and the now familiar site of squat Brueghel-like figures; swaddled old women were bent in labor over the fields.

"Who are those people?" I asked, looking out at the laborers, all of whom seemed to be old and female.

Noel glanced over her shoulder back at me as we rattled and bumped down the last of the gravely stretch to the stables. "Those women?" she said brightly. "They're peasants."

"Peasants?" I said.

My mother laughed softly.

"We don't have that in California," I said.

"You don't have peasants in California?" Noel said.

Lily laughed louder.

"No." I shook my head. "You never see anyone who looks like that."

"You won't see them much longer here either," Noel said. "They're dying out."

"They're closing the washhouse in Haut de Cagnes," Lily said informatively and Noel nodded. "Yes, it's sad. The old women won't have a place to gather and gossip anymore."

"It's so sad it's closing." My mother sighed. "We're losing a sense of community."

"You want to go there and wash your clothes?" Noel said and Lily shut up, having never set foot there. We drove into a stone courtyard surrounded by rows of stables. Two outdoor riding rings, one with jumps in it, were on the outside of the courtyard and stables bordered by open fields.

Kathryn and Anik were already there and came over to greet us. Kathryn introduced Noel and Lily to the trainer, a portly man in jodhpurs and cap. They ignored me. The trainer talked with Noel in French while Lily and I listened, and then after a lengthy and animated conversation finally looked at me and stretched his hand out.

"American!" he announced.

"*Oui,*" I said. I didn't speak French well, but was confident with this word.

Noel then explained in French that I was an experienced rider, that I had my own horse back in America, and had been riding for years. True enough, we lived in Malibu Canyon and I rode in the Santa Monica mountains. Western style, on trails.

"Ah!" The trainer exclaimed.

Two teenagers were standing by, watching and listening, an attractive tomboyish girl with short, dark hair and hazel eyes wearing a black turtleneck, jodhpurs, and tall leather riding boots, and a lean, blond, athletic boy in a sweater, cap, and likewise in jodhpurs and boots.

"Allo!" the girl said to me and the boy nodded. They were a team. We all shook hands.

"Allo," I echoed.

After another extended conversation between Noel and the trainer, it was decided that I would ride Flash.

"Flash!" the French girl said, the one in the black sweater. I looked at her and saw that she was bothered.

"*Oui,*" the trainer said curtly.

The boy looked at the girl, then shook his head as if in disbelief, and the girl left to get Flash out of the stable. The boy followed along and the two muttered in discontent between themselves.

Ten minutes later, the girl came out with Flash and we watched her saddle him and then lead him by the bridle, all the while gently talking to the horse, her head close to his nose. Kathryn glanced briefly at me with a blank, odd look and whispered to Anik. Then they left to ride in the beginner's class. Their duty was done.

Flash was not a large horse, but was solid, well proportioned, and delicate in appearance at the same time. He was golden brown with a long, thick, black mane and tail, and black stockings running up his legs. The horse was proud and shook his regal head at the sight of us. The whites of his eyes showed as he threw up his head snorting and looked down and sideways at me. This was a high-strung horse.

"Is that a stallion?" Lily asked. Lily knew horses; she had grown up on a farm and I could tell this horse made her nervous.

Noel took a quick look under the horse's belly and said something to the trainer. "Yes," she reported.

Lily was eyeing Flash, who had started to prance. The horse did not want to stand still and the girl held the bridle tight and the horse's head close, talking softly and trying to keep him calm. "What did you tell them?" Lily said. "That horse looks wild."

"I told them she's a great rider," Noel said.

"*Oui*," the trainer said and nodded, looking pleased and then said something else we didn't understand.

Lily looked worried.

"He says all Americans are great riders," Noel said.

"Cowboys!" the trainer said.

"Cowboys?" said the girl holding Flash and smiled despite herself. It was obvious she didn't think this was a good idea. She motioned to me, then held tighter to Flash as I approached and mounted.

When she let go, Flash immediately reared up on his hind legs and pawed the air. I leaned forward, holding Flash's mane, then sat back in the saddle when Flash came down, seeing the image of my mother's frozen face pass by my line of sight. Noel was silent and watching apprehensively, as the horse lunged forward and the group fell back and got out of the way. The horse danced around in a circle, and I gained control, sitting strait and tall on the horse. The trainer clapped his hands.

"Yes!" he said triumphantly and then called out something in French.

"He wants you to do the course!" Noel hollered. "Do you think you can do it?"

I took my attention off Flash for a moment and looked over at the course. It was a fairly difficult course of jumps laid out in the larger of the riding rings, and I could see that some of them were definitely a challenge. My blood rushed.

"Yes!"

I headed for the ring and they followed and situated themselves along the side, hanging on the white wooden railings. The trainer went into the center of the ring and started barking out commands, none of which I understood.

I managed to complete most of the course with Flash rearing and foaming at the mouth, dashing, stopping, sweating, over-excited and barely controllable. I was exultant, feeling the rush and the power of Flash under me, every cell of my being in tune with the this animal lunging into the approach to the jump, then the lift off, flying through the air, up and over, and then landing, I raised up in my stirrups as his hooves hit the ground. This was heady stuff on this foaming, sweaty beast . . .

The riding master signaled for me to stop and dismount. I was feeling victorious as I stood there and then noticed the girl in the black turtleneck watching jealously. She wanted to ride.

"Yes, Yes. You can join the class." He nodded.

The girl came over and quickly took Flash from me and mounted the horse.

"They want you to watch her do the course," Noel said.

I moved back to the fence to join my mother and Noel, and just at that moment a kitten ran into the riding ring and hid by the brambles attached on a jump, crouched in fear in the sudden awareness of the snorting, chomping horse waiting to run. Flash pawed the ground, sweating rivulets. His rider held him back and then he reared again.

"Wait!" I yelled. "There's a cat in the ring!"

Flash pawed the ground and shook his head, trying to escape the bit as the rider held him back. Flash reared.

"What?" she called out, struggling to hold the horse.

"A cat in the ring! There's a little kitten in the ring!" I yelled. The girl struggled with the horse, and we heard a pitiful mewing from the center of the ring.

"Okay! Get the kitten!" she called out in her broken English.

I dashed into the ring, picked up the poor little thing, and cradled it in my arms. Back at the railing, while holding the cat, I watched Flash repeat the course.

Lily let me bring the stray kitten home, despite Noel's objections, and as it turned out, I not only got to start riding lessons that day but also a pet kitten. I was to get a different horse to ride. Flash was not to be my horse but remained with her regular rider, and I got a horse named Paprika. Lily and I named the kitten Siggy.

Chapter 12

Christopher was nervous as he welcomed me into his house. His grandmother hovered in the background. She had a phony smile plastered on her face, a smile that stretched tightly across her teeth, a smile made with an unnatural effort that resulted in a grimacing effect. I greeted her politely and looked away. I recognized a familiar troubled look in the old lady's eyes, a look I had seen on Christopher, and here it was now in his grandmother's eyes, camouflaged by her glinting glasses.

She ushered Christopher and I into their kitchen, a cozy, dark room that made me think of the dimly lit room in the Van Gogh painting "The Potato Eaters." I liked the effect; it was like a hobbit hole. A teakettle whistled on the stove and grandmother tended to it, pouring boiling water into a china tea pot, then setting it on the round table in the middle of the room.

"Sit here," Christopher said, motioning for me to sit at one of the simple wooden chairs. He turned to the counter and picked the cups and saucers to set them out.

He motioned at his grandmother to move away, and she went to the doorway and stood for a minute with a puzzled look on her face, a hovering presence.

"You have everything you need?" she said.
"Yes. Thank you, Grandmamma."

Reluctantly, dutifully, she left.

Christopher laid out two long baguettes and a plate of butter and jam. He placed a plate in front, then broke off a piece of baguette for the both of us.

"Eat!" he said.

He poured tea into his cup and spooned in teaspoons of sugar, then he spread liberal amounts of butter and jam on the bread.

I imitated him and bit into the baguette and jam. "This is good!" I said.

"Uh huh." He was eating fast.

"We don't have tea like this in America."

"No?" he said, pausing between mouthfuls. "Why not?"

"I don't know, we just don't. We don't have baguettes and we don't drink tea."

"You don't drink tea?" Christopher's voice was high-pitched and sounded slightly imperious, as if this bit of information was almost unbelievable.

"Well, I drink tea, but not like this, after I get home from school."

He took a huge bite of bread, swabbed with large amounts of butter and strawberry jam. "That's terrible!" he said emphatically. "I'm glad I live here."

"It's not all bad-," I said a little defensively.

"But still, I'm glad I live here where we can have this."

I watched him eat the baguette and jam for a moment, then took a big bite of my own. I thought it over. "Yes, this better. You are right."

We continued on in satisfaction.

"So, I went horseback riding, Christopher. We went to a stable and I rode a horse named Flash—"

"His name is Flash?"

"Yes. I jumped him. The horse was wild! When I first got on, he reared —" I put my bread down and pawed the air to demonstrate. Christopher chewed his bread and eyed me.

"Oh yeah?"

"Yes! Flash is a stallion! Stallions are always more wild—"

"You rode a stallion?" he said, eyeing me and chewing.

I nodded vigorously. "Do you know how to ride?"

"I rode a camel once," he said.

"You did?"

"In Egypt. My mother took me to Egypt and we rode camels."

"In Africa?"

"Yes. And I rode an elephant," he continued.

"An elephant?"

"Where? In Egypt?"

"No, here."

"You did not—"

"Yes, I did, at a circus. You don't believe me?"

I didn't know what to believe. I watched him take another huge chunk of baguette and jam. "Oh, a circus elephant—"

"Yes, and after I rode him, I held him by the tail and twirled him around above my head and threw him back to Africa!" he elaborated.

"You did?"

"Yes! Back where he came from!" He nodded and we started laughing and laughing, and his grandmother poked her head in the room and we became quiet. She backed out and we finished eating and clattered noisily up the stairs to his room.

The old lady came to the stairwell and said, "Are you finished in the kitchen, Christopher?"

"Yes, Grandmamma, thank you!"

Grandmamma. The phrase echoed in my mind.

"Keep the door to your room opened," she said.

I looked down at her at the bottom of the stairs and saw a suspicious, sad look on her face and my stomach fluttered. She didn't like me. I followed Christopher into his room and he turned and carefully set the door slightly ajar.

"Why did she say that?"

He sensed my discomfort, scowled, and shook his head. "She shouldn't have said that."

"Why did she?"

"I don't know." He was embarrassed. "She doesn't trust me."

"Oh." I shrugged.

"She can't tell me what to do," he muttered. "She's not my mother."

I dropped it. His grandmother was not so important as to get distracted from enjoying my visit with Christopher. I spied on the wall a poster of Jean Paul Belmondo, the famous French film star, with a cigarette dangling from his lips. I had recently seen one of his movies, *That Man from Rio,* with my mother in town and I had fallen in love.

"Jean Paul Belmondo! I love Jean Paul Belmondo."

"He was really good in *That Man from Rio!*"

"Yes, I love that movie."

"Oh yes, Jean Paul Belmondo. He is the best." We beamed at one another, and our connection to one another was deepened. We sat down side-by-side on the bed and Christopher showed me his hard-cover comic books, *The Adventures of Tin Tin.*

"I've seen those. I like them," I said. "We don't have them in America."

"No?" he said. He pulled out his large collection, then suddenly put them aside, as if he was embarrassed. We shared a sloppy kiss, an anxious kiss with an ear to any movement coming from downstairs, and it wasn't very long before we heard the footsteps coming up the stairs.

His grandmother pushed open the door and peered into the room. The silence must have gotten to her. Christopher was already up and moving about the room, putting his *Tin Tin* books out of sight.

"Christopher, your grandfather will be coming home soon."

"Okay." He nodded.

"It's time for you to leave," he said bluntly as soon as she left. I nodded; I liked this quality of directness in him. He pulled a book down from a book shelf, *David Copperfield*, and handed it to me. I stood up to go and took the book.

I never saw or met Christopher's grandfather; apparently, he wanted nothing to do with any of Christopher's friends, ever, and it was apparent to me that Christopher's living arrangement was not a happy situation. It wasn't completely articulated in my mind but there was an underlying awareness, communicated by Christopher's comments and movements, and those of his grandmother. Christopher was an inconvenience. It was as if Christopher had disrupted his grandparents' lives in what should have been their peaceful golden years in the South of France. They were stuck with a kid when what they had wanted was peace and quiet. There was a shadow hanging over Christopher.

He escorted me to the front door and his grandmother followed.

"Goodbye," I said, turning and facing her at the door, wanting to be liked, wanting things to be right in this house.

"Goodbye," she firmly said. She looked dour and sad and stretched her lips into the smile grimace again, baring her teeth. Then she shut the door firmly with an air of relief, leaving me standing there staring at the shut door.

"So how was it?" Lily said.

"We had baguettes and strawberry jam," I said. "It was good."

"Strawberry jam? That sounds good!"

"Yes." I smiled. Then I said, "Christopher told me he twirled an elephant over his head and threw it to Africa."

"He said that?"

"Yes."

"He has an imagination!"

I laughed and was glad. Lily liked Christopher and that was good.

"I don't think he likes living with his grandmother," I said.

"No?"

"No, he doesn't seem happy there."

"Well, it must be hard for him; his mother left him there."

"She did"

"Yes," Lily said, nodding sadly. "She just went off and left him there, his grandparents didn't really want him—"

"How do you know that?" My voice was sharp.

"Noel told me." She said. "She said his mother went off with someone and just left him."

I was quiet. I felt badly for Christopher, not only because his mother left but that it had been a subject of gossip. I didn't want to discuss it anymore with her and besides I could tell that she had other things on her mind. She had a look on her face and I could tell something was up.

"What is it?" I said.

She paused. "We're going to move in with Noel."

"Oh good. I love her house—"

"We're not moving into her house. We're moving into the downstairs apartment."

I had gone through the downstairs of Noel's house the first time we visited and remembered it as an abandoned and empty cellar, dank and dark and full of cobwebs.

"No! I don't want to live there. It'll be too cold!"

"I'll fix it up."

"Noel said it floods in the winter! I want to stay here—"

"We're moving," she said. "I need to save money."

We had been there for a month and the funds were not unlimited. The move was meant to be.

Chapter 13

"Le Cave," as christened by Lily, could be accessed from the street by walking down wide stone stairs to Le Cave's door below street level. The door itself was thick wood with a round top similar to the kind of door one would pass through to enter into a hobbit warren, I imagined, or a dark hovel.

Walking into Le Cave from the outside stairwell was literally like walking into a cave, or a cellar. There were no windows or outside light, thus the name Le Cave. It had a bathroom on the left of the entryway, down a few steps and off the fairly large main room with a huge claw foot tub. The main room itself opened up under an arched ceiling, or closed in, you could say. The corners of the ceilings curved inward like in a wine cellar. The floor was cement.

An opening from the main room led into a small room at the front facing the garden. This room had a small window and a door that led out to the garden and another opening that led into a small kitchen. One had to pass through this room to get to the kitchen or the garden. This was to be my room.

I wanted as little to do as possible with cleaning the place up. I didn't want to live there, and I made this clear so Lily did most of the work, probably out of guilt. It was as if she wanted to prove to prove to me it wouldn't be so bad, and make it nice.

She discovered that men, quite often drunk, used the stairwell off the street into Le Cave to relieve themselves as they passed by, and after we moved in Lily made it her mission to put an end this practice. She would burst out of the door and chase them away with a broom, yelling in her bad French at the startled men who tried to get away as fast as possible while fastening their pants. One of the first things she did was wash the stairwell and steps with soapy water. Then she went through Le Cave and washed it down completely, mopping and swabbing the floors and walls and the corners of the ceiling Then she started painting. She painted the whole inner room white, and then the cement floor a deep blue. Then she painted the bathroom lavender.

"Do you like it?" she said, about the lavender bathroom.

I went into the bathroom and took a look around. I giggled. "Yes."

She had gotten tired at a certain point or run out of paint. One wall was still yellow. The corners were sloppy.

"It's not finished!" I said.

"I ran out of paint!"

"Oh."

"I'm tired of painting," My mother said. I was still in the bathroom, looking at the giant tub. It was going to be nice to take a bath in it.

"Do you think I should get some more?" she said about the paint.

"Nah." I shrugged. "It's okay like it is." I felt a pang of guilt for not helping her more.

Lily put a single bed for herself against the wall in the large room to work as a couch and bed and set a coffee table in front. She acquired two wooden wardrobes, one for her and one for me. And then she enlisted me to help her with the small room, my room, and we painted it a chalky white with deep blue trim on the sashes around the windows. She put a desk and chair for me to study next to the wardrobe; there was just enough space. I needed a desk because I was going to start school soon in Cagnes at a middle school at the foot of the hill.

The last room Lily fixed up was the kitchen. She cleaned and painted the kitchen and set up a small table and chairs for us to sit and eat .She hummed and hawed about what color to paint the floor and settled on burgundy. The work was finished.

The overriding question in the back of both of our minds, especially Lily's, was how this was all going to work out when the rains came. It was unclear just how watery and dank it would be to live in Le Cave through the winter. Noel had warned her. Nevertheless, my mother got the place cleaned and painted and furnished before the end of September, our first month in Haute de Cagnes. It would be ready for us starting October.

Chapter 14

I ventured out on my bike to see the surrounding countryside, gradually expanding the perimeter of my territory outward until eventually I rode off the hill. On the north side of the village, the side facing Nice, was a road that switched back and forth down the steep side of the hill to the lush valley below. I rode my bike down the road and turned inland to ride along the river. After a while I got tired and pulled off the road, stopping in a shady glade by the river.

Looking down at the rippling swift currents of water and then up at the arbor of trees sheltering me, I felt really good. I felt embraced and sheltered in this place, this glen. I felt safe. It was late autumn, and there were an abundance of leaves on the ground; there had been a recent rainstorm. There was an unfamiliar softness to the edges of the trees and leaves—the brown, golden, green, and red leaves bleeding together on the ground and emerald shoots of grass sprouting up. It was as if the invisible particles in the air were damp. This was what I noticed when I realized I loved Noel. I was struck by the intensity of my emotion, by this feeling of love for

Noel, and by the beauty surrounding me, and I then I thought about the difference between this place and the countryside in California where I spent so much time in the Malibu mountains near Los Angeles. It was dry and crystalline in those mountains, brittle, not soft and old like this place.

I thought about my father and brother and that I loved them and missed them, but missing them was diminished in loving Noel and having her in my life. I thought about the Malibu mountains back home and the coast of California, how beautiful it was with its sharp edges, and this place here by this river in France that was old, but not quite yet ancient. I sensed that something had happened in this place where I was standing, a thousand footfalls that had tread here and stopped just as I had and looked at this swift river. Unknown people that felt what I was feeling, close by, people like me who might have been thinking about love and beauty and missing someone. *Maybe I will love women like my mother,* I thought, and I thought about her drinking and the fear I had felt in London, and that it had never left me. I retraced my mother's and my journey to the banks of this river.

We had driven north into the English countryside when we left the bed in breakfast in London. I was looking out the window at the green rolling hills and English pastureland, and Lily started talking about Druids. We were headed for Stonehenge, and she was trying to prepare me, but she didn't know much about the Druids except that they wore long robes and performed mysterious rituals in the English countryside at Stonehenge and that they were probably extremely spiritually elevated and enlightened beings.

"Are there Druids there now?" I had asked her.

"No, not anymore—"

"Why not? Where are they?"

"I think the Christians killed them."

"They did? Why?"

"I don't know." Lily shrugged. "Maybe because they practiced magic."

"They practiced magic! That's why they killed them?" My voice sounded shrill.

Lily was uncomfortable with the way the conversation was turning and had a pained look on her face. She nodded and shrugged. "I don't really know."

I had mulled this over, thinking about Druids in long robes and conical hats, waving wands around, and then I looked out the window noticing the hugeness of the sheep on the hillside.

"Mom! Look how big the sheep are! They're huge!" I was trying to lighten the mood.

Her binge and my fear were with us like a hangover, and the talk of dead Druids didn't helped.

Lily had taken her eyes off the road for minute, glancing past me.

Huge, wooly sheep grazed on the neatly sectioned plots of land separated by hand-built rock fences into tidy blocks. It was lush and green, with a gray cloudy sky behind the giant sheep peaceably grazing.

"You're right, they are huge," Lily said, and we laughed.

Then Lily had said. "It's always gray in England."

But not always. The sun poked out at sunset and the sky cleared as we approached Stonehenge. Jutting up out of nowhere on flat pastureland, we spotted the mysterious rock columns in the afternoon twilight. The site was practically deserted when we arrived and we had it to ourselves.

A cold wind blew over the sloping land and through and around the columns, as we wandered through the stones. Lily found a perfectly aligned spot to watch the setting English sun through the columns and called me over. I stood and looked, and my mother grew bored and wandered away. I was imagining robed Druids standing in the very spot where I was standing, and then I felt as if there were beings living nearby in the darkness behind or inside the fading light of the day that I inhabited. They were inside and living in a velvety blackness. I stood in the wind, not minding the cold at all, and watched as the sun met the land, coming down through the sky and then sink below the horizon, and encroaching darkness unfold. My mother was silently watching me from across the circle until she finally called out. "It's cold!"

She went for the car. I could have stood there longer, perhaps a thousand years or more, perhaps forever, and lose track of time, but she had distracted me and I noticed the cold. My mother moved toward the car and I followed her. She turned up the heat once inside and we rubbed hands together.

She didn't feel what I felt at Stonehenge, and she wouldn't feel what I was feeling here in France by this river, I realized. There was a gulf between us. She didn't acknowledge this mysterious space, and she rejected the idea of god. But there was more to it than that, so much more. She had brought me here and loved the beauty here. She loved life and you took the good with the bad, and when traveling the good usually won out due to the excitement of the new. She gave me this.

I left for home, for Le Cave, feeling a sense of peace and acceptance. France was my home now. I rode my bike back on the same windy road I had come down on in the twilight and quickly discovered the downside to riding off the mountain. You had to get back up it. I pedaled slowly up the switchbacks as far as I could, which wasn't very far at all, and walked the bike the rest of the way.

Chapter 15

"Do you know how people have sex?" Christopher asked.

Christopher and I were walking along toward his house on the north side of town. On one side was a fortress-like wall with lookout windows high above, and on the other side the wall fell away toward the valley buttressing the cliff. Down below, the river sparkled in the sun.

I looked over at him, and I could tell he had given this some thought.

"Yes," I said.

"That a man puts his—" He looked embarrassed and didn't finish the sentence.

"I know," I said.

"They take off all their clothes," he added with a sly look.

A smile crept onto my face; I was amused at his embarrassment. "Yeah, so?"

"Well," he hedged, "I was thinking we could try it."

"Christopher! We're too young!"

"We aren't too young!" he said. "We could do it if we wanted. Why do you think we're too young?"

I shrugged. I didn't know. "I don't know. You have to be older."

We walked along silently a few paces. He was working up to something.

"Do you want to do it?" he finally said.

Surprised, I looked at him. "Have sex? Do you?"

"Yes. I want to have sex," he said most decisively. He waited a moment. "Do you?" he said. "Do you want to have sex?" Now that he had said it once, he could say it again easily.

We walked along and I thought about it.

"Do you want to have sex?" he repeated.

It might be fun, I thought, *to try.* The idea suddenly appealed to me as a mission of discovery.

"Yes," I said.

"You do?" he blurted out. "You want to have sex!?" Like, he didn't believe me.

"Yes, I want to have sex," I said.

"You have to take all your clothes off," he said.

"I know."

"So you're going to take all your clothes off?" he said, unbelieving.

"You have to, too. Are you going to take all your clothes off?"

"I will if you will."

We went up to his bedroom in his house. Thankfully, we were alone; his grandparents were out.

"We have the place to ourselves. She's gone," Christopher said. His grandfather was out of the picture as usual, he wasn't even mentioned.

We sat down awkwardly side by side on his narrow bed, and Christopher pulled a mitt and baseball out to show me.

"I have an American baseball," he said.

"Uh huh." I was all about having the sex.

We lay down and started to kiss, and then separated and lay prone on the bed.

"Are you going to get undressed?"

"Are you?"

"I will if you will."

I unbuttoned the top two buttons of my blouse, and Christopher unfastened the button on the top of his pants. His hand went into my blouse and I waited breathlessly. He quickly pulled it out and lay back. We lay there in a long awkward pause, and neither of us moved.

"Are you going to take your clothes off?" Christopher said.

"You first."

He propped himself up on his elbow.

"You first."

"You."

More pregnant silence.

"This isn't going to happen," he finally said.

Secretly, I was relieved. "I told you we were too young."

"You're right," he said. "We're too young." He sat up and slumped over in a dejected pose.

"I expected you to be more like James Bond," I said, sighing. I sat up and buttoned my shirt.

"You expected me to be like James Bond?" he repeated back in a chirpy high-pitched tone.

"Yes. That way it would just kind of . . . happen," I said.

"You mean you wanted me to do all the work!" He sounded truly indignant. Then a moment later, he said, "Shhh," and put his fingers to his lips.

We heard the sound of the front door opening and shutting.

"Christopher?" His grandmother was at the foot of the stairs. "Are you up there?'

"Quick, get up," he whispered and jumped up, fastening his pants. I quickly buttoned my shirt. We heard her footsteps coming up the stairs and she pushed open the door.

"Hello, Grandmamma," he said. He was up and moving around the room.

She looked at me with suspicion. I sat innocently on the bed.

"Hello," I said.

"Hello," said the dour, old lady. She sighed and went back down the stairs with an air of resignation. This was a new development coming home to find the boy alone in the house with a girl. Christopher stood in the middle of the room looking perplexed after his grandmother left.

"She wasn't even mad," he said.

"Christopher! What if she had come home and found us having sex?!"

"Yeah", he said. "Good thing we didn't do it."

On my way home I felt disappointed that we hadn't had sex, but relieved at the same time. Still, I couldn't get the idea of it out of my mind. Yes, I finally decided, we were too young, but still, it seemed like a missed opportunity. Christopher confused me.

Chapter 16

Christopher got it in his head we should go
on a bike ride and was exuberantly enthusiastic
about it. It was going to be great fun! We would
do the loop around the river in the valley and
stop at a candy store on the far side, a store that
Christopher was fond of and eager to share with
me. I agreed and we met up at his house on or
bikes and then started the descent down from
Haut de Cagnes. He quickly took the lead on his
racing bike and made it off the mountain down
the switchbacks in no time at all. He was show-
ing off. He waited for me at the bottom.

"Slow down, I can't go that fast!" I said.

"It's my bike, it's because it's a racing
bike," he said, looping in small circles as he
waited.

He took off again on the road by the river
and was soon far ahead. When we got to the glen
that I recognized, I stopped.

"Wait!" I wanted to stop in the familiar spot.

Christopher looked back over his shoulder
and looped around the road again in tight circles.

"Let's stop here!" I yelled.

"On the other side!" he yelled back impatiently. We'll stop on the other side!" He wanted to get to the candy store.

I caught up with him, and he took off, getting far ahead again. I peddled furiously to keep up and he turned around and snickered, then stopped and waited.

When I caught up he took off fast again and I gave up. I fell back into my own pace until Christopher was barely visible in the distance. He waited for me at the end at the bridge where the road turned and goes back.

"You're going too fast," I said.

"It's hard for me to go slower; I have to keep a pace, that's how I peddle."

"Christopher!"

"Okay, I'll try to go slower."

We rode together until we came to a stone building with a sign hanging out front with elegant black lettering painted across the front window that read: "Confectionaries."

"This is it!" he said.

The shop was musty and strange to me. It seemed like the shop must have been there a hundred years or since World War I, I was thinking, and the candy sitting in the glass jars that long as well. I preferred the modern and gleaming rows of neatly packaged American candy. Familiar candy.

Christopher excitedly picked out several of his favorite candies and gave one to me. He watched me as I put it in my mouth. I took it out after a moment and put it back in its fancy wrapper.

"I don't like it," I said.

He frowned and pointed out some other candy, hard sour balls. I was thinking about Big Hunks and Ju Ju bees, Twinkies and Rolos. Suddenly, I missed all the candy that I knew and loved, and suddenly I was homesick. These strange sour balls and confections didn't compare at all, not with what I loved at home, and I didn't like the store or the girl behind the counter. I liked the stores in America much better and suddenly I yearned for them.

Christopher was watching my face. "What's wrong?"

"Nothing," I said.

"Let's go," he said, stuffing candy in his jean's pockets.

We stopped at a clearing by the river, and I watched as he stood there eating candy next to the water's edge.

"My mother is going to put me the school in Cagnes Sur Mer."

"She is?" He sounded surprised.

"Yes. The fifth section."

"We'll be in the same class," he said. I watched his face as he turned this bit of information over in his mind and he was glowering. I could tell he didn't like it.

"You don't want me to be in the same class as you?"

"I didn't say that." He quickly said. "It's just that it'll be different, it won't be the same--"

"Why?"

"With the other people there—"

"What do you mean? You mean your friends?--"

"Yeah – They—" He got flustered. "It'll be ok!" The conversation ended.

"This is my favorite. Here," he said.

He pulled a wrapped candy out of his pocket and held it out to me, but I shook my head.

"You don't like the candy, do you?"

"No."

He stopped eating and we stood there together and stared silently at the water and the river swirled and rushed by. The moment was pregnant, and I waited for a kiss.

Christopher looked at me. "You're waiting for me to kiss you aren't you?" he said indignantly, his voice high pitched.

I didn't say anything, taking note of peevish incredulity written on his face. I didn't understand what the problem was.

He stared at me and I didn't say anything, and shame started rising up in me.

"You were, weren't you?" he continued on accusingly. "You were waiting for me to kiss you?" As if I was committing a crime.

I nodded. "Yeah, so?"

"Well, I don't want to kiss you. I want to eat my candy," he said, sealing the matter. He pulled a piece of candy out of his pocket, the same piece I had refused, and put it in his mouth. We stood there, him sucking the candy, and the sound of the rushing river became very loud to me.

"C'mon, let's go," he finally mumbled. He pushed his bike over the stubby field and climbed on it and rode away. I followed him and watched as he pedaled fast down the road not looking back, as if he was making an escape. I got on my bike and followed after him, watching as he became a small figure in the distance and then disappeared completely. He didn't wait.

I walked my bike back up the switchbacks to Haut de Cagnes, confused and angry. It was the beginning of the end with Christopher.

"Why didn't you wait?' I asked him later.

"Oh, the bike ride?" he said. "You were going too slow."

"You should've waited for me!"

"Yeah, I should have waited."

Chapter 17

I started middle school in Cagnes at the bottom of the hill. On my first day, I stood at the front of the room and the teacher introduced me to the class. I ducked my head, shy to be standing at the front of the class, and when I looked up rows of students were staring at me in curiosity.

"*Bonjour*, Suzanne," they said in unison. What a strange, old-fashioned place this was!

The students sat two to a desk with the girls on one side and the boys on the other. I saw Christopher sitting toward the front of the room with a familiar-looking boy, one of the boys who was with his gang on the first night that I had met him. I looked right at him, but he wouldn't look back and his face was blank. Then the teacher walked me down an aisle and sat me down in an empty seat next to a girl whom she introduced as Marcie.

Marcie was a dark, pear-shaped girl with beautiful, delicate features and doe-like eyes. Her pretty face was framed by curly, dark-brown hair. The teacher asked Christopher to come over and translate. He reluctantly got up and came over and stood next to me.

I looked at him. This Christopher was a different Christopher than the one I was familiar with; he was a pale and slouched over in bad posture, and his shirttail was un-tucked and hanging loose. He was disheveled and utterly unengaged with himself and his body and with me. He hung his head as if to say *This is who I really am and now you know.* I was astonished. It was hard to believe this was the same boy that I knew, the boy full of energy and wanting kisses.

"Hello," I said, studying him.

"Hi," he mumbled, looking at the floor. Marci glanced at him and then away; he was pathetic in her eyes, that was obvious. The teacher didn't have any patience for his diffidence and started in on him rapidly with a set of instructions, none of which I understood.

"She wants you to copy from her book since you don't write French, okay?" Christopher said. Finally, he looked at me and I could see that his face was dark with anger. "Okay," I said.

Marcie moved her hand off her notebook, revealing lines of elegant cursive script filling up the top half of the page. Impressed by the cleanliness and neatness of Marci's book, I put Christopher and his troubles out of my mind.

"You don't mind?" I said to Marci.

"Yes. Yes. It is all right," Marcie said in bad English.

"*Merci.*"

Christopher stood there awkwardly, smelling boyish. He needed a bath.

"Go sit down," the teacher said, and he slunk back across the room to his desk. I watched him as he crossed the room, trying to be as unobtrusive as possible. The teacher returned to the front of the room and shuffled some papers on her desk.

"I am glad you are sitting here with me," Marcie whispered.

"*Pour quoi?*"

"The other girl who was here before. She stinks," Marci explained in her stilted English. She made a quick motion, holding her nose with her index finger and thumb to demonstrate the girl's stinkiness, and motioned at a girl sitting a few rows in front of us. An awkward-looking girl in a dirty, ill-fitting dress, a dress she had outgrown and whose hair was snarled and unkempt, turned around and glowered at us.

I looked at the girl. I had seen this before. There was always one misfit girl or boy in every class, and this was the French version. It was the same as the American version, an unfortunate soul who was despised and picked on and you felt sorry for, but you didn't get involved. At least I didn't' you didn't want the stigma to rub off, especially if you were new.

I nodded to Marci. This was to be the start of a friendship.

On the break, the girls gathered on one side of the playground and the boys on the other side. A group of girls gathered in a ring around me, chattering and curious, and Marci stood next to me, proud to have this new American girl as her friend. Nicole, a tiny and diminutive young girl, beautiful and dark, welcomed me with a giant smile.

"We are very glad you are here," she said.

"*Merci.* Thank you," I said.

I was watching Christopher out of the corner of my eye, but he was ignoring me. He was roughhousing with his gang of boys, and I could see they were secretly eyeing me back. They stopped playing and a boy I recognized came over to me, the boy who sat next to Christopher.

"The American girl is very beautiful," he stuttered in bad English and then backed away embarrassed as the girls watched. Christopher was also watching and passed close to me.

"Hello!" he said and his eyes were laughing. I felt relieved to see he was friendly and happy, and then the boys fell away and retreated to their corner.

I loved my school supplies. I liked the stack of blue notebooks and the leather satchel. The satchel was well made and substantial and the handles felt good in my hand. The buckle on the flap was easy to open and the latch satisfying to operate. There were separate hardcover blue notebooks for each subject, one ink pen and black ink, graphite pencils, as well as a set of colored pencils, a sharpener, and a handy pencil box in which to keep them all, a ruler, a protractor, and a triangle. I learned right away that it was extremely important to keep the notebooks neat and write in as fine handwriting as possible. This was a highly valued skill and on the first day of class I made a large, black blot with the ink on my first attempt with the pen and ink. There was an ink well and ink in a small recession between myself and Marcie on our desk, and I watched as Marcie dipped her pen and proceeded likewise.

Marcie looked over and watched as a large, black inkblot spread on my notebook and looked alarmed. With great concern, she showed me how to dip the pen in the inkwell and write without blotting the paper.

I carried my notebooks in the brown leather satchel, which I took to swinging on my way back and forth from school at the bottom of the hill, and back up to the top of the hill to our new home at Noel's. The swinging satchel aided my gait, especially going downhill, which I did once in the morning, and then back up at noon for a two-hour lunch break, and then back to school at two in the afternoon and back up at 5:00 p.m.

At home in Le Cave, I'd set my satchel down next to my desk and set up my notebooks for writing and homework. I'd take out the pencils and the pen and ink and perhaps do a neat shaded drawing or measure out some geometric figures. Lily would stop and look over my shoulder. She was secretly as impressed and enamored with the notebooks and pens and pencil boxes as I was, with the orderliness of it all.

Chapter 18

It wasn't too long after I started school that a gang of boys appeared in the street outside Le Cave. Lily and I were in Noel's living room when we heard the commotion, a cacophony of yelling and excited shouts followed by whistling.

"What's that noise?" Noel called out from upstairs.

"I don't know," Lily called back. She walked over to the staircase and looked up to see Noel standing at the top of the stairs in her pajamas and robe. Noel had been having a bout with her illness and had finally gotten out of bed. It was late afternoon.

"How are you feeling?" Lily said.

"I feel fine," Noel said.

Lily was relieved that she was up and feeling better. It was a challenge living with a person with cancer, never knowing how she sick would be, the ups and the downs. Lily was walking on eggshells.

Noel disappeared from the top of the stairs. "It's a gang of boys!" She yelled. She was in the bathroom, looking down at the street She came back and called down to me.

"I think they're here for you." She started laughing, and Lily and I were relieved to see her laughing and happy.

"Come up here!" Noel called out, and ran back to the bathroom. "Bring a bucket!"

"A bucket?"

I rushed into the kitchen and looked all around.

"There's no bucket!"

"Bring a pan! Something to hold water!"

I grabbed a large saucepan off the counter in the kitchen. I ran upstairs and joined Noel in the bathroom, who was filling a bucket with water and we were all laughing, the house was full of giggles. Noel and me upstairs and Lily downstairs.

"There's a gang of boys in the street!" Noel screeched.

The boys looked up at the window to see who it was, their voices shouting and drowning one another out.

"Fill the pan!" Noel barked.

I filled my pan with water.

Noel tossed water out the window from the bucket onto the boys down below, and there was more yelling. I tossed water from my pan and we laughed and re-filled the pan and the bucket and tossed more water. The boys' voices became subdued and discontented. They moved away from the window, drifting away down the street and then out of sight.

"What's wrong, Christopher?"

No answer.

I was riding my bicycle alongside Christopher, who stared straight ahead. He was pretending I wasn't there. He hadn't spoken to me for days, and Lily suggested I take his book back as an excuse, as a ruse to get him to talk to me. I had *David Copperfield* in a basket on the front of my bike.

"What's wrong?" I repeated.

His face flinched just a bit; it was obviously an effort him to ignore me, but he kept doggedly walking along, silent.

"Why won't you talk to me?"

He was walking fast, but it was still hard to ride slow enough on the bike alongside him, as the front of my bike wobbled. I straightened the bike and continued on.

"Do you want your book back?"

Finally, he stopped. He stared at me. "Yes."

"Why won't you talk to me?"

"You threw water on me!"

"I didn't!"

"Yes, you did. I saw you."

"That was you? With those boys? I didn't know you were out there."

"I *saw* you!" he said. "You looked down out the window."

I knew it was true. I had been caught up in the moment laughing with Noel, and when tossing the water I might have caught a glimpse of him, but he was just another boy among the gang. But it was Noel who doused him, definitely not me.

"I'm sorry. I didn't know you were out there. I wouldn't have done it if I'd known you were out there."

"I don't believe you." Christopher looked straight ahead again and started walking again. "You looked straight at me," he said.

"Do you want your book back?"

He stopped and turned towards me. He held out his hand, and I handed him his book. He started walking again, and I tailed him, wobbling along on the bike.

"I finished it," I said. "I liked it."

Christopher ignored me and continued walking, and I gave up and circled my bike back around and rode away. It was over.

Chapter 19

Lily and I arrived for dinner at Marie's. Marie lived in an apartment up and over an incline on the same narrow street that we were on, a street that ran across the complete length of the village and then angled in a sharp left to join the main village road. I walked both of these streets every day on my way back and forth to school, the main road running up from the foot of the Cagnes to the castle at the top of the village and our road. For fun, I often rode my bike on our street up the hill and raced it down it on the other side past Marie's house.

The two us had returned to eat at Marie and Jean's restaurant many times since our first visit, Lily more times than I. She liked to drink in the bar there. I could only imagine the night she sat at the bar drinking and commiserating with Marie, who was going through the breakup of her marriage, Lily talking about the dissolution of her own relationship back in California as best she could in her poor French, and the two of them falling into empathetic silence with one another.

Lily might mention that I was homesick and missed my father and brother and that it was Thanksgiving in America soon, and that it would be particularly hard for me. Lily, sitting and smoking and drinking in the bar in Marie's restaurant, explaining the American ritual of eating turkey with their families on this special holiday, and again emphasizing how I was very homesick. Marie nodding sympathetically and pouring herself another drink—it was past closing time by this point—and then graciously offering to have us over for the evening on the special occasion, the "American" holiday of Thanksgiving and offering to prepare a turkey-themed meal. Marie explaining that she herself was also sad because her husband, Jean, had finally done it, he had left her and she was now alone in her house. It would be nice to have the company. I imagine this melancholy conversation was accompanied by a few discreet tears (knowing my mother) and was difficult since Lily's French was extremely limited and Marie's English even more so.

An invitation was extended by Marie and my mother left the restaurant, grateful, yet apprehensive and Marie came away with the general idea that turkey must be on the menu for this dinner, a dinner she had somewhat impulsively invited us into her home for. They had both been drunk when the invitation was extended and accepted, and had second thoughts upon parting.

We arrived on Thanksgiving night at Marie's front door, and Marie shepherded us into her home. I looked down at the immaculately clean and polished red tile floor as we stepped into her spare yet tastefully decorated room with whitewashed walls. The room had a somber cavernous feel to it and the mood was gloomy. Marie was full of false cheer.

"Sit down. Sit down," she said and waved her hands to a long wooden table laid out with three place settings.

Jean had left and his absence was palpable. Lily had explained the situation to me, that they had separated, on the walk over, and it was fresh in my mind. It was on all our minds.

"Happy Thanksgiving!" Marie said, stumbling over the words and looking sad.

"Thank you," Lily said. I forgot about Jean and our conversation; I was thinking about turkey.

I sat at one end of the long table and Lily in the middle. Marie disappeared from the room and then returned moments later carrying a casserole.

'What is that?" I said. "Are we having turkey?"

Marie and Lily both registered surprise.

"The turkey is in it. Casserole," Marie explained and placed the casserole on a mat in the center of the table.

"Oh," I said, obviously disappointed.

Marie sat down and looked pointedly at me. "You don't like it?"

"I thought we were having turkey. It's just that it's not what we have for Thanksgiving in America. We—"

A dark cloud gathered on Marie's face that soon turned into indignation. She quickly dished out portions of the casserole."Don't be rude!" Lily said. "You're not in America, and Marie has gone to the trouble to prepare this meal for us."

"I'm sorry." I looked from face to face, then down at the table. Then I picked up a fork and started quickly eating. "It's good," I said.

It was too late. I had ruined things and Marie was insulted. She didn't get over it. We ate in silence, mostly. There was an attempt at conversation, stilted by the mood and worsened by the fact that Marie didn't speak good English and Lily didn't speak French. It was all so much more difficult for them without the lubrication of alcohol. I was quiet. When we finally left, after an unhappy dessert, it was none too soon.

Lily and I walked silently down the road back home.

"I'm sorry I said that about the turkey and Thanksgiving. I think I ruined the dinner," I said.

"That wasn't very much fun was it?'

"No." I shook my head.

"It's okay," Lily said after a moment. "She's just unhappy because her husband left her. It's not your fault."

I felt a rush of relief and then fear—a large sewer rat scampered by and down a storm drain. It was at least a foot long.

"Did you see that?" I said.

"Yes!" Our senses were wide awake now and we moved to the center of the street, forgetting about the dinner at Marie's.

Up and up the hill I pedaled on my bike, slowly and laboriously.

"Allo, Madam!" I called out to a thin, middle-aged woman carrying vegetables in her net bag. A baguette poked out the top. The woman had a colorful headscarf holding back her graying hair and was heavily made up; she was a fading beauty. She lived a few doors down from us and I passed her often on the street.

"Allo. *Comment allez vous?*" The madam smiled magnanimously at me. She liked me.

"*Je suis bien! Et tu?*"

She stopped and frowned at me, staring at me in disapproval. Then she looked perplexed for a moment and smiled slightly and turned away. I had somehow offended her but had also been forgiven.

What was it? I thought to myself as I pedaled slowly up the incline with an uneasy feeling in the pit of my stomach. And then it came to me that I had used the familiar instead of formal phrasing in my French. *Ah well,* I thought, *this incident was not so important in the scheme of things, French is complicated.* I dismissed it.

At the top of the hill, I paused for a moment anticipating my run down the other side, anticipating the rush of the speed, feeling much better. I barreled down the street with the wind on my face, my long hair whipping behind, and in my exultation thought briefly of the incident with the madam and thought, *I'll remember to use the formal next time!*

I couldn't see around the corner, the road curved around the side of the mountain into a narrow lane with barely enough room for a car to pass through, and I always hoped for the best, expecting it would be clear, and it was. It was great fun to go fast down that road! This was my new favorite ride having gotten bored with the ruts and jumps of the main plaza.

Chapter 20

Marcie and I became friends, sort of. We had little in common and it was a friendship of circumstance rather than one of mutual attraction, but nevertheless in those first days we pursued the relationship with enthusiastic curiosity. Everyone and anyone French within ten years of my age range was enamored with American pop music at that time, and Marci was no exception. It just so happened that I had been collecting rock 'n' roll records, something I had started in California and continued in France; I had found a shop that sold them in Cagnes, and Noel had a phonograph. I invited Marcie to come over and listen to records.

We spent an afternoon in the corner of Noel's living room where Noel kept her record player listening to Bob Dylan. Marcie wanted to know the lyrics. For hours, or so it seemed, I stopped and started the record, specifically on the song "The Ballad of the Thin Man" over and over, right after he sang, "Do you Mr. Jones?" to catch the preceding phrases. I would then repeat the lyrics in English to Marcie, who was scribbling thoughtfully. For those unfamiliar with this song, it was not particularly uplifting and was sung in early Dylan's monotone nasal twang. I hadn't noticed this quality in his singing before this session.

"Do you Mister Jones?" filled the room with its somber tone, and Marcie nodded for me to stop the record. I picked up the needle off the phonograph, politely obliging her, then glared at her pointedly. I had repeated this at least five times. Marcie was oblivious and continued diligently recording the lyrics.

After several more times, Marcie stopped writing, to my relief, and asked what the lyrics meant. I attempted to explain the meaning of Bob Dylan's lyrics, not knowing what half of them meant myself, and then we fell silent.

Marcie looked over her notes and then at me with a perplexed expression, perhaps something had gotten lost in translation? Noel came in and looked at the two of us ensconced in the corner.

"Why do you keep playing that over and over?"

"She wants to know the lyrics to the song," I said. It was obvious that I was exasperated. At that point Marcie recognized the frustration in my voice.

"Well, stop it, please," Noel said.

I looked at Marci.

"It's okay," Marci said. She set her lyric sheet down and looked morosely at the floor.

"Thank you." Noel left the room.

Soon after this visit, Marcie returned the invitation and invited me to come to her house for her family's noon meal. She lived in an apartment in the flats of Cagnes close to the school.

The meal at Marcie's house was no less than a feast by any standard I had ever known. Marcie lived with a large extended family. The women were all dark and stout, and the men were working class and ruddy, with noontime shadows on their faces. Their voices were loud and boisterous and the laughter constant throughout the meal, filling up the room.

After seating me next to Marcie at a large dining table, already crowded with china and silver and napkins, wine and water glasses and pitchers and bottles, Marcie's family took their seats and the meal commenced. Marcie's mother and grandmother carried in large platters piled high with pasta, huge bowls of greens, bread piled in baskets, and a platter of fish, and they set all this food on the table. The women kept bringing in food until the table was completely loaded down and filled up, covered with huge mounds of vegetables, fish, pasta, bread, red wine, and water.

I felt small in my seat looking at the loaded table and the food in front of me. Marcie's mother smiled and her father greeted me and asked a few perfunctory questions, and then the men proceeded to converse loudly among themselves. I was a skinny, little, American girl with large eyes.

There was a problem. It was the platter of fish. Whole fish had been fried and piled on a plate, and Marcie's mother had placed it so that the fish heads were staring at me. I noticed it immediately after the platter was set down in front of me—the dead fish eyes looking at me, the fish lifeless and splayed across the platter stacked in a pile.

I looked around the table, forked down a couple of bites of pasta, and then my eyes wandered back to the fish faces and fish eyes looking at me. I lost my appetite. I could barely manage to eat much at all with the dead fish corpses piled up and watching me, and then the laughing voices got louder and louder. I kept looking at the fish laying there in death.

"You don't eat much!" said Marcie's mother in French or Italian or whatever it was she was speaking, somehow the words were intelligible. I managed a weak smile. I noticed that Marcie had packed away a hefty meal. She was sitting quietly satisfied with her hands folded neatly across her belly resting in her lap. She had her eyes on her mother, anticipating being excused from any cleanup chores because she had a guest.

"*C'est bien*," I said softly and smiled. "*C'est bien.*"

I felt bad I didn't eat more and was grateful when Marcie rose from the table and took me to her small room at the back of the apartment.

I liked to eat bread and honey and in fact marveled at the food in France, how it tasted better than the food back home. The milk tasted better, the bread tasted better, and the honey tasted better. Everyone knew and understood that the bread was better—it was baked fresh every day, but I couldn't figure out why the milk and honey tasted so much better. What was the reason for that? Obviously, there was something very wrong with the food in America. Why the vast difference in these simple things?

"The milk tastes better here. Why?"

"They pasteurize it America," Lily said. "It takes the flavor out of it and they don't do that here."

"They don't?"

"I don't think so."

"So why do they do it there?"

"To make it safer."

"It's not safe here?"

"I think it's safe. They do something different."

"Why don't they do that in America?"

Lily shrugged and smiled. "I don't know. Maybe to save money. It's just better here."

"And the butter, it's different—"

"It doesn't have salt in it," Lily said.

I didn't dwell on these particulars. I started collecting different types and strains of honey for taste comparisons. Now that I was in Cagnes, in the flats almost every day for school I had access to more shops. I tried dark honey, medium and light honey, and honey with the comb. The honey with the comb utterly fascinated me as it had been unattainable in America, where I was from anyway, and I had never seen it before. I took the jar and examined the comb in the golden hue through the glass, dipped a bit of the honey onto a baguette, chewed, and the pulled out a section of the waxy comb and nibbled.

Chapter 21

The entire class walked single file in a line through Cagnes, the girls first, followed by the boys and led by the teacher. There was a feeling of anticipation in the air. We were excited and we laughed and talked and shouted with one another as we walked through the center of town. We felt more alive being out the classroom! We walked from the school down to the main boulevard of Cagnes, down the tree-lined street past the shops, and past the café where the older teenagers hung out, students from the Lyceum, the college prep high school. I remembered back to that first day when Lily and I had passed by this café and the self-conscious shyness I had felt. It seemed like so long ago and now I was a part of it. I was part of this world.

It was a beautiful day and we were going for physical education at the park in the middle of town. The park had a ball court that the boys immediately took over and an area with gymnastic equipment where the girls gathered.

The trees were dripping leaves, and the girls waded and kicked through the golden, green, and red clumps on the ground, under a canopy of twisted dark branches. The exercise pits were filled with sand and clean and clear. They had been freshly raked. I stood in front of a rectangular long-jump pit, filled with sand and with meter markers etched into the cement along the side. Marcie was by my side watching.

I was enthralled by this sandy pit, and I looked long and hard at it. I had never before had the opportunity to see just how far I could jump. I backed up, all the while looking at the pit, then ran fast and jumped as far and hard as I could.

After excited chattering followed by a careful examination of the markings and calculating and measuring the distance I had jumped, I motioned for Marcie to go. She shook her head no. She didn't like physical exercise, she explained, and she didn't want to try. I asked her again, I cajoled her, but she still refused. Nicole was watching from the rings nearby and she came over and challenged me to see who could jump the farthest. She was small, but fit and athletic, and she won. Laughing, she went back to the rings and invited me to join her. Marcie frowned and I declined, wanting to stay with my friend, but feeling a whisper of discontent, wanting to go play with Nicole. Then the teacher left and most of the students dispersed, and Marcie and I were one of the few remaining in the park. I lingered, wanting to cherish this moment—this day felt precious and the jumps exhilarating, and the color of the leaves and the trees so beautiful. Marcie and I walked across the overgrown, deep-green grass through the leaves kicking piles and talking, comparing France and America and their respective physical education programs. We walked out of the park and into town.

We walked back to the main boulevard, the same way we had come, and there was Anik across the street with her gang of friends at the café. The older students had been let out of the Lyceum. Anik turned and waved at me and came over to us. She kissed the air on both sides of my cheeks and breezily greeted me. I kissed her back, and Anik pulled back and looked surprised. Somehow the kissing had not been performed correctly, and I had committed a social faux pas. I had not kissed the air and simply touched cheeks; my kisses had landed on her face with a smack.

I ignored it and introduced Marcie to Anik, who brusquely said hello, barely acknowledging her and then turned away from us. I felt mortified. I wondered if my greeting kisses were so improper, what with my lips contacting skin, or if it was Marcie that was the problem, or both. Marcie and I stood silently and watched Anik, who was now flirting with a handsome boy in a leather jacket leaning against a Vespa, her back squarely facing us.

Dispirited, we walked away from the older teenagers.

"How do you know her?" Marcie asked.

"Her mother is a friend of my mother's," I replied. "She goes to the high school here in town, the Lyceum."

"Oh," Marcie said.

I looked at Marcie, who had become unhappy. Perhaps because she didn't do the long jump? It couldn't be that, I thought; it was something else, perhaps the encounter with Anik.

"Are you going to go there next year when you go to high school?" I said.

"No," Marcie mumbled.

"Why not?"

"I'm just not. I'll go to a different school."

"But you should go there; if I'm here I'll go to the Lyceum."

"My parents won't send me there," Marcie said flatly and then she looked at me—her eyes seeking and suddenly tragic. I dropped the subject. We parted quietly at the next intersection. Clearly something was going on here that I was unfamiliar with.

Feeling sad and confused I wandered back down a side street, wanting to avoid Anik on the main street, and passed by a shop. It was a photography shop and in the window was a photograph of Marie and Jean, a picture of them on their wedding day. I stopped in front of the window and examined the photograph. Marie was looking up at Jean with an adoring look, and Jean, dressed in tux and ruffled shirt, looked down at his new wife like a lovesick puppy in mutually adoring solicitation. I was struck by the staged romanticism of the photo, the sickly sweetness of it, and then bleakly thought *They are divorcing.*

Chapter 22

Months passed and my mother and I embraced our new life, but we didn't settle into a routine. My senses were too completely engaged in my surroundings for it to be routine. I expanded my explorations further a field and rode my bike on long rides in all directions from the bottom of the hill on my free days off from school.

The little port in Cagnes Sur Mer by the sea was a slice of life that was on the cusp of forever changing and disappearing. It was a small port filled with small fishing boats, colorfully painted in accents of red, green, and blue. It was pretty far for me to be at the port, but one afternoon I rode down there. Perched on my bike, I stopped and looked down at the sea and at the sun pooling and reflecting off the water.

This is so beautiful, I thought dreamily, and then slipped into a reverie as I listened to the lapping of water against the wooden boats and the pier and gulls cawing and circling above me, feeling the warmth of the winter sun and the breeze, and inhaling the salty air tinged with a fishy odor.

There were a couple of old fishermen in fisherman caps and dirty blue work clothes, folding and pulling nets, smoking and gossiping. They were men who had lived their lives fishing from these small boats whose way of life would soon come to end in this place and I knew it. This place was so old and quaint, and the one high rise in the distance was what was to come. I pedaled slowly through a side street when I saw him. A boy, my age or a little older, with striking blue eyes, black hair, and dark, tanned skin, as if he spent a lot of times outdoors. I had noticed him before in Haut de Cagnes in dirty work clothes and had stared at him curiously. *Why is he dressed in those clothes?* I wondered and he had stared back at with a blank expression, his face impassive.

I was looking at the houses on the street, small, white houses with trim of red and blue, like the boats in the harbor. The streets here by the port were bare compared to the streets in Cagnes proper; there were no trees but just narrow sidewalks and the cozy whitewashed houses. The late afternoon sun created blocks of shadow off the window sashes and off the tiled roofs and there was a rich melancholy feel to it. I was relishing the feeling and pedaling very slowly. Out of the corner of my eye, behind me, I saw the boy jump on a bike that was in lying in a yard in front of one of these little houses and pedal after me. He was following me.

My mood shifted immediately from reverie to nervousness. The boy was behind me on a bike and keeping always the same amount of distance behind. I turned down a side street and looked back over my shoulder; he appeared round the corner when I was halfway down the block, the same distance behind, watching. He was playing a game. I slowed down, so did he.

This game made me nervous, but now I was enjoying it. I kept pedaling at the same pace and the boy did also, never trying to catch up. Then I took off fast and pedaled up toward Haut de Cagnes and when I turned around he had stopped and was just watching. He circled back, turning around and rode back toward the port.

"I went to the port today," I said to Lily that evening.

The cat, who had grown much larger and fatter, was sitting on the sill of my room cleaning her paws and Lily was cooking a small dinner in the kitchen. We weren't eating with Noel this evening like we did most evenings, but in Le Cave.

"What port?"

"In Cagnes Sur Mer, there's a port down there. It's beautiful!"

"Is there? You went that far?"

"Yeah."\

"I didn't even know it was there," Lily said, stirring and frying something in a pan.

"A boy followed me on my way home."

"What boy?"

"I've seen him here in Haut de Cagnes before; he has black hair, blue eyes, and is maybe a little older than me. Do you know who I mean?"

"No." Lily was frowning. "Did you talk to him?"

"No," I said. "I got scared."

"He shouldn't follow you," she said. "Don't go that far any more. Don't go to the port."

"It was nothing, he didn't really scare me—"

"Don't go down to the port by yourself!" Lily said.

"All right."

I rode the other direction next time. I rode for miles down the highway between Cagnes toward Antibes and finally stopped at a café that faced out to the sea. Once seated, my bike propped next to me on the outdoor patio, I ordered a plate of raw oysters. I sat there in the sun by myself, facing the sea, waiting for my plate of oysters and feeling glorious. This was a beautiful place, in this wonderful world, and I was going to eat as many oysters as I wanted. I was on top of the world.

The proprietress, an attractive middle-aged woman, stood in the doorway of the café watching me eat the oysters. Perhaps it was a bit unusual that an American girl would ride up on a bike and sit by herself and order a plate of raw oysters and then eat them very quickly with a dash of lemon and salt. Perhaps. She had a slightly concerned look on her face as she watched me enjoy my oysters, and perhaps she knew something that I was unaware of, and wouldn't have been surprised at all that I would ride home and make it back just in time to the toilet and violently throw up.

Chapter 23

Paprika was a gray mare dappled with red, brown, and black spots and had an ornery streak. I could empathize; after all, she was bridled and saddled and then cinched up tight around her belly. Somehow the whole thing was just unacceptable for Paprika, and she refused to get used to it. She'd bloat her stomach to keep the cinch loose when saddled, and I'd watch the stablehand knee her in the belly, and then Paprika's ears would lie back in extreme annoyance as she exhaled. After this indignity, she was expected to stop and go and jump on command with a rider on her back. That was a lot ask of anyone or thing. My own horse back home had a similar stubborn streak; she'd been "broke" by a mean cowboy and it took years for her to gentle after the rough treatment. I understood Paprika's resistance, and Paprika responded to my gentle lead . . . most of the time. That's how it is between a rider and horse, it's intuitive. The other part of the time, Paprika would balk. I was just weight on her back and she'd back up, and back up, and back up, as if to just say "No!" This usually happened in the jumping ring.

I would lean in and pet Paprika and loosen the reins and talk to her as she backed up and just let her do it. Then the instructor had what could only be described as a conniption fit. He didn't share any sympathy for Paprika's resistance and wanted his riders to have complete and total control all the time, and kick and hit the damn horse if need be to gain it. He wanted me to kick Paprika in the ribs and switch her if necessary with my riding crop to get her moving forward.

It was frustrating for all of us, for me, for Paprika, and for the instructor. He would start yelling unintelligibly, to me anyway, since I couldn't understand his French, and then he would gesture wildly while Paprika kept backing up.

He generally stood at edge or the middle of the ring, out of the way of any potential lunging horse. He just looked ridiculous when he waved his arms around, comical if you will, and in my opinion was taking it all too seriously. He looked like he was about to have a heart attack. He was a heavyset man, and standing there in his jodhpurs and high leather boots, his large stomach protruded out, adding to a comical effect. His face would turn dark and red as he got increasingly upset. First, he would swat his pant leg with a switch he held in his hand, a sign of things to come, that escalated into wild gesturing and yelling, and ended with him pulling his cap off his balding pate and throwing it to the ground. This he would do when he was utterly exasperated.

The horse would put her ears back flat against her skull and get a mean look. I would glance at him as he yelled and gestured, louder and louder, and then finally I might relent, which I did on this particular day. I gave Paprika a sharp kick and a light switch to the flank. The horse jumped forward. I leaned in, and after a few more pats and kicks, and soft words, we leaped in and started the course.

She performed wonderfully. Paprika and I were on the wind now, oblivious to that screaming fool-of-a-man off to the side of the ring, the riding instructor. I was only aware of the mass of muscle and movement of the horse underneath me and the energy of Paprika's mind down through the reins as we started a slow approach to the first jump. We did a tightly controlled gallop to the jump, and then Paprika was up and sailing effortlessly over with a loud snort. The landing was perfect.

After the next couple of jumps, the horse had worked herself up into a frenzy. This was where I had to be careful and keep Paprika reined in so she'd get the approach right. The frothing animal and rider, Paprika and myself together approached the jumps in a controlled clip. Leaning in, I loosened the reins, and we sailed up and over, clear by inches every time. We did a tight galloping loop back around for the second set of jumps on the course, and then the final set of jumps, which included the highest of all. I held Paprika in and approached the highest jump on the course, second to last, clearing it with ease and then took the final smaller jump. The course was finished.

Paprika and I pranced in triumph. When the horse circled around and we were facing the instructor, I saw him throw his hat on the ground. Then he stalked out of the ring scowling and loudly muttering.

I put Paprika away. The horse was all sweetness now, ducking her head for some petting and nuzzled me. We had an understanding, me and the horse—we knew we had done the course magnificently.

"See you next time, Paprika," I said and went over to the ring to watch Anik and Kathryn in the second form. I had been coming every other week, catching a ride from Haut de Cagnes with Kathryn and Anik, who were in the class behind me called the second form.

This class simply trotted the horses around in a ring single file while they learned how to post, followed by a short gallop. The horses were at a fast trot as I came up to the ring and I watched Kathryn trying to post, her body stiff and leaning forward, rising up and down in rhythm to the horse trotting. She was unsuccessful at posting, and it was painful to watch. Her rump kept falling at inappropriate times in the trot cycle back into the saddle and then bouncing back up. She had a grimace on her face. I looked away and at Anik, who looked absent, as if she would prefer to be back in town on a Vespa with her boyfriend and not horseback riding at all. Soon, they would finish and we'd head home together.

I looked past the two of them out at the fields and copse that lay beyond the ring. I longed to ride out in the countryside on the trails and dirt roads and explore the countryside like I did back home, but it just wasn't meant to be.

"Do they ever go outside the stable?" I asked Anik as we pulled out of the stable and headed for home. I was in the back seat of their Citroen and Anik was in front with her mother.

"Oh yes. They go out on the trail." Kathryn eyed me in the rear view mirror.

"I'd like to do that," I said.

Anik turned around and smiled at me. "But you are jumping!" she said.

"Yes, it's really fun," I said and fell back and looked out at the window. "The instructor got angry," I added.

Anik turned around and smiled again. "He did?"

"Yes." I nodded and slipped into a reverie. The countryside was bare and brown, with dark green rows of vegetables in fields, and gnome-like figures were bent over working. I suddenly felt the passing of time. *Winter is here*, I thought. I was overcome by the bleak, soft beauty of the landscape, and then thought of my brother and father and then the screaming voice of the riding instructor. Tears filled my eyes.

Kathryn looked back at me again in the mirror and murmured something to Anik that I didn't catch.

"It's not important!" Anik said softly. "Don't pay attention to him."

Chapter 24

"Did you know Christopher from before?" Marcie whispered.

We were in class, sitting side by side at our desk.

I nodded yes.

"You and he—"

"Yes." I nodded again.

"Did you—"

"We kissed," I said. I wondered how Marcie knew; there must have been some gossip.

"It's over now. He won't talk to me," I said.

"He is . . ." Marcie muttered with a shrug of disgust. I didn't hear the last word Marcie said; it was muttered in a low, guttural voice, but I knew it was an insult.

I looked at her.

"There is something wrong with Christopher," Marcie said. "No one likes him."

"Mmmm." I nodded; it was sad to hear her say that.

The art teacher entered the room and I forgot about everything but art class. I loved art class. The teacher fascinated me; he was a bona fide French artist!

Dressed in a suit, with a lank forelock hanging over his forehead, he sat on the edge of desk in a somewhat diffident pose and lit a cigarette. He started his lecture walking us step by step through drawing an orb and then shading it in colored pencils. He was a middle-aged man with an aura of gentle resignation about him, accompanied by a whiff of failure, of a dream not fully realized. After all, he had not made it in Paris and was teaching art in middle school, but nevertheless or despite this, he had the presence of an artist! A true artist, I marveled, art was his life. After class I asked Marcie about him and found out that he lived and worked in Haut de Cagnes. We were neighbors!

"Do you want to go to his studio?" Marcie said.

"Have you been?"

"Yes, he invited us there."

"Yes! I want to go."

The next weekend I went down to retrieve Marcie, and together we walked back up the hill into the village to visit the teacher in his studio. It was a sunny day and we walked slowly, but Marcie had to stop to catch her breath few times. I was in splendid shape; I walked up this hill daily, but it was an effort for Marcie. We were both in high spirits—Marcie liked being a guide, and I was the follower.

Monsieur Painchaud, the teacher, lived on the same street as Christopher, about half a block up on the north side of town in a small apartment next to a bridge that arched over the road. We walked up a narrow staircase to his apartment and my excitement mounted—the bridge, the apartment, the steps to his studio, it was wonderful!

Marcie smiled at me and knocked on his door; she could see I was excited and she was happy to provide this adventure.

"Hello," Monsieur Painchaud greeted us and let us in.

He had been at his easel when we arrived, painting. He put his brush down and sat back on his stool by his painting, lit a cigarette, and smiled. He painted constantly, in the style known as pointillism, and his studio was filled with his paintings. Every area of wall space was filled, and paintings were stacked and leaning against every spare bit of space below.

I stood silently in a small area of his studio and looked at the walls filled with paintings and the paintings on the floor at the front of the stacks. I looked at the washed-out blue dot paintings with shades of green and white, mostly landscapes of the surrounding countryside. The room was filled with painted dots, stacks of dots on dots, and an odor of turpentine. Monsieur

Painchaud sat back smoking and Marcie chatted with him in a respectful tone of voice, and they both watched me. Then we left. I was deeply impressed. *It is a wonderful thing to devote your life to painting dots,* I thought, *a strange and somewhat magical thing to live your life surrounded by your creations of dots on dots.*

Later, I told Lily and Noel about him and described his studio filled with paintings.

"Really?" Lily said.

"He isn't any good," Noel said dismissively. "He couldn't get a show in Paris."

"I liked them," I jumped to defend the Monsieur Painchaud. *Clearly, Noel doesn't understand the significance of him,* I thought. *The man is an artist.*

Chapter 25

I walked slowly up the hill home for the noon lunch break, swinging my satchel. My route had taken took me through the side streets of Cagnes two blocks up Main Street, and then straight up the steep road to the top of Haut de Cagnes. I fell into a rhythm of walking and swinging the satchel, the weight of it pulling me up on the upswing and keeping me alert on the downswing so as not to fall backward and lose my balance. I was swinging and walking, hardly looking around until more than halfway up, but not yet at the bar Tabac, where I took a sharp left. I walked a short distance on a shadowy narrow lane, less than a city block, and then a sharp right on the same street up to the Le Cave.

A boy lived in the house right where the streets converged and often was sitting on his doorway steps where I passed by. He always greeted me with enthusiasm, obviously eager to make my acquaintance and I was flattered, I didn't mind. He was a good-looking friendly boy, about my age, albeit he seemed a little dopey.

"Allo!" he called out.

"Hello." I smiled.

"*Comment allez vous.*"

"*Je suis bien.*"

"*J'mappelle*, Tony."

He always used the formal form of speech with me, always polite.

After a while, I would sometimes stop and talk to him, but on this particular day, I kept walking and continued up the street and went into the upstairs part of the house, into Noel's living room.

When I came into the room, a boy turned and looked at me, a different boy from Tony. It was the boy who had followed me on the bike in Cagnes Sur Mer. He was working with his father plastering the wall. His thick, straight, black hair fell across his eyes when he turned around, and he was tall for his age, tan and fit. We stared at each other for moments. He slowly lowered his arm and hand, which held a tool until his arm lay against his side. I looked at the tool; it was some sort of plastering tool. He was dressed in white coveralls with smears of plaster and dirt on his clothes and white plaster specks flecked his dark hair. He was working with a dark, trim, older man in his forties with deep creases in his stubbly face. The boy and his father were re-plastering a section of the wall in Noel's living room.

The older man kept working silently, smoothing and scraping the wall, and the boy's eyes fell across me, looking at my clothes and at my satchel of books. His face darkened, and he turned away from me back to the wall. His father glanced at him and then at me and said something to him in a soft voice as he continued scraping the wall. I left the room without saying anything and went down to Le Cave. Lily was downstairs.

"That boy working upstairs," I said. "That was him, the one on the bike."

"What boy? What are you talking about?"

"The one who followed me on his bike. In Cagnes Sur Mer he followed me on his bike, remember? I told you."

"Oh, it was him? You don't have to worry about him; he works here in the village with his father."

"How old is he?"

"Fourteen or maybe fifteen."

"Why isn't he in school?"

Lily stopped whatever it was that she was doing and looked at me. "He's an apprentice; he's learning his father's trade. He's finished with school."

"At fourteen?"

"Yes. Not everyone goes on to high school here; they learn a trade instead and they don't continue on with school after age fourteen. They stop after middle school."

"Did he decide that?"

"No," Lily said, suddenly sounding serious. "It wasn't his decision."

"Someone decided for him?" I said. "He should be able to go to high school!"

"But this way, he'll have a skill when he grows up. He'll have a trade," Lily said.

"It isn't fair," I said. "He should go to high school."

"Yes," Lily said and then she looked sad. "That's how it is here in Europe. It's decided if they will continue on in school when they are fourteen, or if they are going to apprentice and go into the trades or not."

I thought about this. "But what if he changes his mind later about what he wants to do?"

Lily shook her head. She looked confused. "He can't change his mind." "He should be able to change his mind! And go to college," I said indignantly.

"It's different here, that's why it's better in America. Young people can choose what they want to do and change their mind no matter where they come from. It's not that way here."

I went and threw myself on my bed thinking about the unfairness of it, how utterly bleak this fact of life here seemed to be, and thought about the boy upstairs, and that he was extremely handsome. I felt sad. Then I got up and went out into the garden. Lily had planted flowers and put a table and chairs out by the wall facing the bay. I sat down and looked out across the land and sea at Antibes. A slight breeze picked up, and I took in the fragrance of flowers and of the sea breeze. My adopted cat was stalking insects through the overgrown grass, and I watched him for a moment. The cat was black and white, and bigger than ever. The cat was in fact enormous. I thought about the boy and his father working up there and looked up at the house but couldn't see inside, the windows were too small. I saw hummingbirds darting around a bird feeder that Noel had put out by the steps. *This place is like paradise*, I thought, *it's so beautiful, but still, the boy upstairs isn't free.*

After that day, I saw the boy around the village a couple of times and he was always dressed in dirty work clothes. We never spoke or acknowledged one another and he never looked at me again.

Tony, on the other hand, was gregarious and conversational. He parked himself on the steps every day, twice a day, timing it so he would be there to greet me when I passed by. He would be at there at noon when I passed by for the lunch break and in the evening hour when I made my final return. Sometimes he would be absent in the middle of the day, and instead be inside eating his midday meal. As much as he liked to be on the steps to greet me, the midday meal trumped these meetings.

Of course I noticed this wasn't just a coincidence. I started to look forward to him being there and our conversations. He was warm and polite, and he made me laugh. I missed him when he wasn't there, and one day I noticed I could see inside his house through a window facing the main street. The window to the room was covered by a fluttering transparent curtain, and Tony and his family were inside eating their midday meal at a large table that filled up the small room. I could hear them talking and laughing, and the clattering of dishes and silver. I imagined what a feast it was that they were enjoying.

"I missed you at noon," I said to Tony later that day. It was 5:15, precisely and he was waiting on the steps. He lit up.

"We eat at noon, I was inside eating," he explained and I nodded and smiled. He jumped up and asked if he could walk with me and I said yes. So we walked up the street toward my house and talked about pop music for a block or so and then Tony turned and went back. I invited him to come and visit.

Sitting in the corner of the room, on the floor, Tony could barely bring himself to look me in the eye. I sat next to him and asked him what to play, what music he wanted to hear, and Tony blushed and looked puzzled. We were having a hard time communicating.

I picked something up to show him and he looked at floor. Then he looked at me and his eyes glazed over. We didn't speak as the music played, and Tony looked around the room, as if he had never seen such a grand place, as if he didn't belong in this place.

"Did you like it?" I said when the music stopped.

He looked at me and didn't answer. He smiled slightly, enigmatically.

I asked again this time in French, and he quickly nodded and blushed, acting as if he was ashamed. Then a long silent moment passed.

"Do you want to hear something else?" I said, and Tony didn't answer. Tony was looking at the rug, a nice rug to be sure, and then Noel came in and gave him a dismissive glance and said something to him in French that I didn't understand.

"*Oui*, Madam," Tony said. Then he smiled at me and looked at the floor again.

Noel left the room and I sat waiting for something, a word or something from Tony, but he didn't speak. He was feeling panicky and I could sense it. I looked at the records and then at Tony.

"Do you want go?" I said.

He quickly jumped up in relief, his eyes on my face so as not to miss a single cue.

The next day, Tony was back on the steps and he greeted me, but we both knew there was no future for us. Tony made a halfhearted and sad effort to talk, but I didn't stop and only said hello and kept walking. He disappeared from the steps after that.

A few days later, I was accosted by a gang of little boys in the street in front of Tony's steps.

"*Tu et fache a* Tony!" a boy screamed. I recognized him as Tony's little brother, maybe six years old, seven at most. I stopped, not understanding what he was screaming about, and he repeated the words again. His little face twisted in anger. I moved away from him and he and his gang, three boys, followed me up the street screaming, and I still didn't understand what they were yelling about, only that it was about Tony and that the boy was using the familiar *tu*.

I ignored him, and he reached up under my dress and grabbed my underwear and snapped it.

The other boys were watching and looked shocked. I twisted away and pushed the boy, then hit him hard with my satchel in the back. It thumped against him, and he jumped slightly, not losing his footing a bit, as if this blow was just another blow among blows. His little shoulders hunched up in a small shrug and the other boys pulled him away. Shaken, I continued home.

Noel was furious when she found out and went down to Tony's house and had a talk with his parents. "They won't bother you again, Noel said when she came back. And they didn't. I never saw Tony on the steps again after that or spoke to him. I saw him and his little brother a few times on the street, and they never so much as looked at me.

Chapter 26.

I hopped on my bike one afternoon after school to go for a ride. I headed out on a familiar route pedaling slowly up the hill near Le Cave, paused briefly at the top, and then barreled down the other side, picking up more and more speed, going faster and faster, the wind on my face, my hair flying, riding in and out of shade and sunlight—life felt very good!

I went fast around a bend in the road, and around the corner there was trouble. Marie and Jean were coming up the road, just the two of them together with Jean at the wheel in Marie's black car. I caught a glimpse of Marie's unhappy face through the windshield and wondered, *Why are they together? Aren't they divorced?* And Marie's face turned from unhappiness to fright as she saw me coming fast toward their car. There was no room to pass because the road was too narrow, and the car filled up the space between village walls.

I veered to the right of the car avoiding a head-on collision, and the bike went into the very small opening between the car and the stone wall of the building on the other side to a scraping stop. I was lodged between the car and wall and had hurt my hand.

Jean rolled the window down, right next to where I was stuck, and simply looked at me. I was examining my hand, which was bleeding.

"Are you hurt?" he finally said.

"It's my hand," I said, flexing it. "It's bleeding."

"Is that all?"

"Yes."

Marie put her hand to her head as if to say "Thank God."

I had scratched their car and bent the side view mirror. I looked at the damage and then back at Jean. "I damaged your car. I'm sorry."

"It's okay," Jean said. Marie's face went dark; it was her car. "The important thing is that you aren't hurt," he added.

"I'm really sorry," I said again. I backed my bike up carefully out of the opening just wanting to make an exit. I backed up until the road was wide enough for them to get through. They edged past me and drove away.

When I got home I didn't tell Lily how I got the cuts on my hand. Not right away anyway, but then I relented since I knew Marie would say something. Lily seemed unconcerned; she looked at my hand and we agreed I didn't need immediate medical attention. Then she started talking about a doctor she had met at the bar Tabac. She was preoccupied by this doctor, a young man about twenty-five years old.

"He can look at it," she said. "I invited him over for tea." Then she added, "You'll really like him. He's really smart and handsome. He wants to meet you."

I looked at her perplexed. *Why? He's twenty-five years old.*

"He's too old. My hand is okay—"

"Oh no, he has a nephew your age he wants to introduce you to, but he wants to meet you first."

"What boy? Who?"

"The boy's name is Pierrot. He's thirteen and he's a lonely boy. He doesn't have any friends, so we thought you two could be friends."

"Mom! I can make my own friends."

"Please, Pierrot really needs to meet friends, please just meet him. You might like him, okay?"

"All right."

"And besides, the doctor can look at your hand," she said.

Why does she want me to meet a doctor and his nephew? I wondered. No apprentices? No Tony sitting on the stoop? Was it Noel? It must be Noel trying to fix me up with this doctor and his nephew.

The young doctor rapped on the door to Le Cave. Lily had prepared tea and pastries and set them out on tray in the garden where we sat in the sun and chatted after the doctor took a quick look at my hand. He turned it over in his palm and then squeezed it slightly.

"It's okay," he said. "It's healing."

Lily was smitten with this doctor, I could see right away. I was unimpressed; he seemed utterly bland. He was a slender man with wavy, golden hair and a pleasant face, dressed in khakis and a button-down shirt with a sweater tied loosely around his neck. He was polite, sweet, intelligent, gentle, and he was very earnest. He was boring.

I sat across from the doctor, my mind wandering. I thought about the Vespa that Lily had recently bought and that I wanted to ride it. I was thinking that perhaps when the doctor left Lily would let me ride it. It was a special event that she had bought it, a Vespa! It wouldn't be long before Lily would let me ride it. Lily and the young doctor conversed. Finally, after what seemed like a very long time, he leaned forward and asked me if I would meet his nephew Pierrot. He was worried about his nephew—Pierrot was lonely and needed friends. It seemed like this had been repeated more than once, and my mother had a concerned look on her face when he said it. I already felt sorry for Pierrot before even meeting him.

"Yes," I said and smiled. "I'll meet with him."

The doctor seemed grateful and stood up with a worried look on his face and said it was time to go. His mission was accomplished. He bowed slightly to me and left.

"I really like him." Lily sighed after he left.

"He's nice," I said, noncommittally.

"Oh, isn't he?" Lily said, her voice aflutter. "You know, I hope you marry someone like him when you grow up."

"You do?"

"Yes," Lily went on. "I hope you marry someone like him."

I knew that never would I ever marry someone like him and my mother and I exchanged looks. I didn't say anything.

Chapter 27

Pierrot was a slight boy, dark, good looking, and well dressed with a cowlick that added to a general demeanor of a sad, young Jiminy Cricket. The two of us, Pierrot and me, sat facing one another in his house in Haut de Cagnes, sipping tea out of china teacups and nibbling cookies. Our faltering conversation was interspersed with awkward silences accented by the ticking of a large clock. My eyes kept straying from Pierrot's anxious face to the clock on the wall behind him. I had my eyes on the long hand, anticipating the click as it jerked forward.

An attractive woman in her twenties brought in the tea. I watched her as she glided into the room carrying a silver tray loaded with the tea service. She brought in hot tea and sugar, served in flowery fine china and dainty cookies piled neatly on a plate. She emptied the tray onto a small table between Pierrot and myself, then cast a sideways look at me, discreetly scrutinizing me. I was examining the little table that was between me and Pierrot; it had intricately inlaid woodwork of a chessboard on it. I was about to ask Pierrot if he played chess when I raised my eyes and caught a glance between the woman and Pierrot and recognized that this woman knew Pierrot better than anyone. They were intimate in a secret way. I lost my train of thought. Pierrot dismissed her in a curt, soft voice and she left the room noiselessly, shutting the door softly behind her, trying to be as quiet as possible.

"Is she your maid?" I asked, my voice sounding loud in the silence.

"Yes." Pierrot nodded and his eyes glowed. There was a trace of smugness in the way he said "yes" and in the way he looked at me when he said it, but his demeanor was amiable and inoffensive. It was just that he knew that he had something that I didn't have, a personal maid. He had been to Le Cave and seen where I lived; the doctor had brought him there for an introduction.

"My father is gone a lot," Pierrot explained about the maid. "She is here."

"He leaves you alone here?" I said.

"He goes away on business." He nodded. "And I am alone here. I don't have any friends," Pierrot said. His English was stilted, which added to the overall effect of his statements, that yes, this was an unfortunate state of affairs and he looked sad, but he didn't try to hide it and wasn't embarrassed about it. He was guileless.

"But we can be friends?" Pierrot stuttered in his bad English. "And I will have a friend." The situation could be corrected; it was all so logical.

I nodded. "Okay."

I looked at the chessboard on the table and asked him if he played chess. I told him that I had learned to play and that perhaps we could try a game, and he said "Yes!" enthusiastically, and then we fell into silence again.

I looked behind him at the long hand on the clock, and it jerked forward and then back a tiny bit and the clock ticked. The maid came in and started to clear the little table. We sat in silence a bit longer. The maid got a concerned look on her face and as if there was some signal between them, Pierrot stood up.

"Next week?" he said to me with an uncertain troubled look on his face.

"Yes," I said.

Pierrot smiled in relief. The visit was a success!

The maid escorted me to the door and searched my face before shutting the door very quietly.

On my second visit to Pierrot's, he took me for a tour of his house after we finished our tea. I was relieved to get up and move around. We had sat again in front of the ticking clock on expensive furniture and drank tea out of the delicate cups and silver tea service. The maid had again slid noiselessly in and out and waited on us, and our conversation was as stilted and the silences as awkward. The noise of the ticking clock started to seem ominous to me.

The living room was gloomy and elegant, furnished with large wooden furniture and expensive rugs. It was long and rectangular with whitewashed walls and the ceiling in middle was the height of both floors, like a loft, and crossed with large supporting beams. An open staircase on one side of the room ran up to the second floor. Pierrot and I had our tea in a side nook toward the front of this room, a nook where visitors were vetted before being invited into the interior. There were no windows; it was dark and had an aura of muffled gloominess and silences.

Pierrot led me through this room, and we stopped in front of a large, comfortable-looking leather couch and chairs.

"This is where we sit when my father is here," Pierrot said, and I looked down at the empty arrangement. The two of us stared down at an indentation on the plush and comfortable-looking couch and I imagined a full-size man sitting there. I imagined Pierrot's father sitting there, and a feeling of aching loneliness came over me. This was not a happy place.

I didn't know what to say.

"You don't sit here when he's not here?" I said, finally.

"No," Pierrot explained. "Only when he is here."

He moved on, and I lingered and looked at paintings on the walls, and objects d'art tastefully placed around the room. His father collected art. Pierrot went to the stairs and waited, wanting to show me his room upstairs.

His room was a small room and he had a cradle for a bed. We stood together in the middle of his room and once again stared down at the furniture, at his little bed.

"You sleep there?" I said, puzzled by the cradle.

"Yes," Pierrot said. "I sleep here."

It had wooden sides all around and could fit a large child.

"It looks like it might be too short," I said.

Pierrot looked thoughtfully at his cradle and didn't respond. It was neatly made up, with the bright, white sheets folded, tucked-over blankets, and a plumped-up pillow. There was not a wrinkle anywhere. I took my eyes off the bed for a minute and looked around the room. There was no rug on the floors or pictures on the walls; nothing was out of place in this room. The floor was immaculate without a trace of dust on the red tiles. It was cold.

Pierrot was still staring at his bed. "It is small," he said in his stilted English. He observed it with a serious expression.

I laughed. "Do your feet fit?"

"Oh, it fits!" Pierrot said and then turned to me and we both laughed. It was unusual and a relief to hear the sound of laughing in that house; I could tell by the way it echoed and it didn't last long. Pierrot didn't know if I was laughing at him, but it didn't matter, he was willing to give me the benefit of the doubt. We went back downstairs and the maid looked glad; she had heard the laughing. She was going to show me out but Pierrot spoke softly to her, in that familiar and intimate curt voice, and she quickly disappeared behind a door. He escorted me to the door.

"You'll come back?" he said at the door, holding it ajar, his eyes still shining from having laughed. He was more assured now.

"Yes."

I thought about Pierrot and his strange, gloomy house on my walk home. It was dark and I looked over at the bar Tabac as I passed by and could see it was full of people. I caught a movement out of the corner of my eye; it was a giant rat. It skittered along the side of the street and across the cobblestones, then slithered down into a rain gutter. I watched it, frozen and standing still in the street, as it disappeared down the dark hole, and then I continued warily on up the street, my eyes scanning the road from side to side.

I arrived at 3:00 p.m. at Pierrot's house, right on time for tea. Once again we sat in the nook and the maid brought the tea and cookies. She smiled at me, and I was about to smile back, but she turned her face away. I was thinking Pierrot and I could play chess today and was about to suggest it . . .

"I like you," Pierrot announced.

The maid silently disappeared behind the door, and I heard it softly shut behind her.

"I like you, too," I said.

"I mean, like boyfriend-girlfriend? You know?"

"Like a friend," I said.

Pierrot took a cookie and bit it off. "I mean, I like you. Like a boy likes a girl. You understand?"

I looked perplexed. "No, I don't understand," I said.

Pierrot put the cookie down and stood up. He was agitated. "A boy likes a girl, like that. You understand?" he said.

"No," I said and shrugged. "I don't understand." I was playing dumb.

"You don't understand?" Pierrot said, looking at me with sad eyes. He sounded a little sarcastic.

"I'm sorry," I said. "I don't understand your English. Maybe if I spoke better French—" The truth was I did understand but didn't want to say so. I didn't want to say no to him, but I didn't want to be his girlfriend either. Then I knew I didn't want to come here anymore. We finished our tea in awkwardness, though it could hardly have been any more awkward than it already had been. Pierrot was upset and trying to hide it.

When the maid came back in the room, she took one look at Pierrot and that was enough. She escorted me quickly to the door with a concerned look on her face.

"The doctor said you pretended to not understand, Pierrot!" Lily said accusingly. "What game were you playing?"

"He wanted me to be his girlfriend!" I said. "I didn't want to."

"You don't like him?"

"No, I don't like him."

"You don't like him," Lily sighed. There was nothing to be done about it, and she was quiet. Then she said, "Okay, you don't have to go there anymore."

Chapter 28

Christmas was coming and we went shopping for a Christmas tree. It was the three of us—Noel, Lily, and me. We found a tree that fit *just right* in the corner of Noel's living room. It was the perfect size, and discussion ensued between Noel, who was standing in front of the tree, now tucked into the corner, and me, who was sitting on the couch, on how to decorate it. Lily jumped in the conversation from time to time, interjecting with what she thought were pertinent points, and then Noel said we would light the tree with candles and Lily and I fell silent. Candles! It was obvious that decorating the tree here in France was going to be a different experience for Lily and I, and that Noel was going to show us how to do it, and that it was going to be much better, much, much better. There was no more discussion about it. There would be no shiny, round ornaments, no strings of Christmas lights, and no fake silver icicles. Something unimaginable and delightful was in store for us, especially for me—the tree was going to be lit by real candles!

A few days before Christmas, the four of us, Frieda included, decorated the tree. It had to be ready for Christmas Eve. Noel led the festivities, instructing us on how to string the popcorn, and we munched it as we made the strings of popcorn and colored beads. Then we draped the long strands of popcorn and beads on and up and over and around the tree, then affixed some toy wooden ornaments to the branches— closest thing to the way things were done back in California— and then crowned it with a star on the top. Then Noel brought out the little candles and candleholders.

"I've seen a tree with real candles," Lily said. "It's beautiful."

"Uh huh," Noel said.

We affixed the tree with the little candleholders as Noel explained how the tiny candles must be carefully placed so as not to cause a fire. Lily and I put a few up under Noel's close supervision, while Noel did most of the work. Frieda sat back quietly on the couch with her usual enigmatic, small smile, sipping hot cider. She was happy just to watch. When we finished we stood back and admired our handiwork.

"Let's light the candles," I said. I was excited about seeing the little candles lit up. Lily was quiet and playing it cool; after all, she was an adult, but she couldn't hide her excitement. She wanted to light the candles. Frieda looked hopeful.

"We'll light them on Christmas Eve," Noel said.

"But I want to see what it looks like!" I said.

"You have to wait until Christmas," Noel said.

I sat down on the couch besides Frieda, whose smile widened. The tree was beautiful, even without the candles, but I couldn't imagine what it would look like with the candles lit.

"It looks like a tree with big bulbs for lights, doesn't it?" I said.

"Oh, it's much more beautiful than that," Lily said.

"It is?" I said.

"You'll see it," Noel said. "If we light them now, the candles will burn out before Christmas."

I kept staring at the tree.

"Oh, come on, you can wait," Noel said. She went to get me some cider.

"Okay," I said. I gave up.

Christmas Eve started in the late afternoon. Kathleen dropped by Noel's just before it got dark. She was elegantly dressed up in Christmas colors and invited me and Lily to her house. She was having an open house, as were many people in the village. Lily graciously accepted the invitation from her friend. Lily admired Kathleen. She admired her British-ness and friendly formality, and she admired her background as a professional musician. Kathleen had been a concert pianist at one point and played in nightclubs in France during World War II. When Paris fell, so the story went, Kathleen broke out in a rendition of the Marseilles to a roomful of the crying patrons. They had a common bond, Kathleen and Lily; they were Francophiles and in love with France. They had left their respective hometowns with nary a look back—Kathleen from London and Lily from small-town Texas—and now they were living out their dream in the South of France. This, in itself, was cause for celebration, and tonight was a special night; it was Christmas Eve.

Noel was listening in on the invitation and watching; she was keeping close track of us. She was hosting her own event and wanted Lily and me home for her own open house and to be present when her guests arrived. We had to be there for the tree lighting and have time to eat a light Christmas Eve supper, and then meet and greet guests and have time to spare before midnight. At midnight, we would go to the church in the plaza in Haut de Cagnes for midnight mass.

After eating supper, Lily and I set off for Kathleen's. The streets and alleys of the village were bustling with people calling on one another, dropping in from house to house, and wishing us a *Bon Noel* as we passed.

Kathleen greeted us at her door and ushered us in; we were the first to arrive. Lily and Kathleen immediately launched into one of their typical animated discussions, in loud voices. I didn't know why they always talked so loud—perhaps Kathleen was hard of hearing—and then we ate sweet candied fruits with hot drinks. We made a swift exit when new guests arrived.

"Noel wants us home," Lily explained.

"*Non*! Noel!" Kathleen said, looking put out.

"Are you going to the midnight mass?" Lily said.

"I'll have guests. I'm staying in."

Outside, Lily paused. We stood in front of Kathleen's house in the cold night air.

"Do you think she was mad that we left so fast?' Lily said, worried that she had offended her friend.

"It was kind of fast," I said.

"Yeah," Lily concurred. "Well, Noel wants us back. She's going to light the candles." We hurried back down the street.

Noel lit the first candle. She brought a box of matches out, the long wooden kind, and ceremoniously lit a match while holding it aloft. She stood in front of the tree, turning a moment to face her audience. It was just the three of us—Lily, Noel, and myself. She lit a few more as we watched. Then she handed the matches to me, instructing me to be careful. I lit a few candles, and then it was Lily's turn. Lily's face looked like an eager child, like she was about to cry out, "No, me first!" but she restrained herself and waited patiently.

After all the candles were lit, we stood back and admired the tree. It was the most beautiful sight I had ever seen. The tree glowed with the small, amber orbs of the candlelight illuminating the greenery and Christmas trinkets between pockets of indigo blackness, an emanating comforting darkness behind the lights.

"Ooohhhhh."

"Aaaaahhhhh."

Noel was quietly triumphant. This was a special Christmas treat from her to us.

Frieda arrived. Noel jumped up to heat cider and get the sweets out. The party was getting started. Frieda gave a neatly wrapped present to Noel, and an unwrapped chess set to me. Then she flopped down on the couch, fell silent, and stared at the Christmas tree perhaps disappointed that she had missed the tree lighting.

Lando was the next to arrive, bundled in a striped scarf, and lively from the cold and champagne stops along the way. He presented Noel with a package tied with a ribbon. A book. He gave Lily and me a box of candy. He accepted a glass of champagne, unwound his scarf, and we chatted. Miriam and Ken arrived. Ken in green and red, with a little dog on his arm, and Miriam was friendly with Lily for the first time ever. She smiled and greeted me with her usual scowl, but was emoting only good will. Noel's circle was complete; she was surrounded by people who loved her.

Lily and I left early for the church; Noel was still tending to her guests.

Lily was glad to get away. Ken's cloying personality grated on her, she said, and Miriam . . . well, Christmas or not, the woman just plain made her nervous, this I knew. The truth of it was that Noel having all those people around her, people who loved her, might have made my mother jealous, made her feel as if she was just another satellite and diminished in importance. At any rate, it wasn't important, and it felt good to be out in the cold fresh air.

Invigorated, Lily walked quickly up the street with me close behind. It was a short distance to the steps that went up to the next street above. The village walls seemed to close in on me in night shadows—the moon was bright and casting shadows. I stopped and looked up at the sky, filled with thousands of stars.

"C'mon," Lily said. "I don't want to be late."

I caught up with my mother on the stairs, out of the shadows and into the light of the moon, and two skinny men dressed in shorts and t-shirts rushed by, their boney knees pumping, their elbows askew and arms at an angle. They were carrying baskets of bread on their shoulders.

"*Bon Noel,*" one called out.

"*Bon Noel!*" Lily shouted. "Why are you working? It's Christmas!"

"Christmas bread!" a man shouted back. They kept on running with this delivery. We stopped and watched until they were out of sight.

"They're delivering Christmas bread," Lily said.

"It's Christmas bread!" I repeated. I noticed my breath when I spoke, fogging the air. My mother was smiling and we stood looking at one another, thinking about the running men with Christmas bread, the stars in the sky and moonlight shadows, and the candles on the Christmas tree . . .

"I love this place," Lily said. I smiled at her.

"Do you think they were cold?" I said. "They were dressed in shorts."

"I don't think so, they were running," Lily said. She was already on her way to the church. "Let's go. I want you to see the midnight mass."

The church, the Chapel of Notre-Dame-de-la-Protection, was packed and standing room only. Lily took a quick look around, then up at the balcony. She motioned to me, and we went up the narrow steps and found a spot to stand. I took a look around. It seemed as if the whole village was in the church and that the ones who weren't dressed up, the non-religious ones like us, were up in the balcony. To my left I spied Christopher sitting on a chair with his grandmother standing next to him. The old lady looked over at us and nodded hello, and Lily nodded back and turned her attention on Christopher, scrutinizing him for moments. He was looking particularly rosy cheeked and innocent and staring straight ahead. The old lady nodded at me and nudged Christopher who then turned and whispered a hello. I nodded and turned my attention to the Catholic spectacle below. The church glowed in candle-light.

The priest, dressed in red velvet and gold vestments, stood at the front of the church. A choir of boys dressed in white robes lined one side of the church looking like wingless angels. They were singing somber Christmas carols in their clear, high voices. A hush fell over the congregation and two altar boys walked down the aisle swinging incense in a slightly careless manner. The church soon became smoky and sweet from the smell.

The choir stopped singing, and there was a brief rustling among the pews downstairs and shuffling of feet in the balcony. Noel arrived in a gust of fresh air and stood next to us. Her eyes were glittering.

The pipe organ started up with a flourish and then was silent and again there was a hush across the pews. The priest began his sermon. In a high, authoritative voice he spoke, solemnly, and the people heard only to the tone and timber of his words, not understanding a word since it was in Latin. I stared at the old man and his impressive hat, fascinated, and then after a while got bored. I searched the pews down below for familiar faces and spotted Marie dressed in her very best, her head bowed in a pious manner.

Christmas came and went, and on New Year's Eve Noel had another party. It started at her house with eating, drinking, and dancing with her friends, and Lily, Noel, and me ended up just before midnight back in the plaza at the top of the village. Lily had relented and let me come to Suzy Solidor's cabaret, which had been transformed into a dance club. It was the first time I had been inside, and I couldn't see much it since was so crowded with moving bodies, but I noticed the walls were covered with photographs and drawings of Suzy Solidor.

At the stroke of midnight, Lily took me out of the club, but not before I watched a young man, his long hair flying, pick Noel up and swing her around. Noel laughed and he put her down, and he kissed her.

The three of us walked back home. We were giddy as we walked back to the house, and secretly glad that the parties were finished. Lily was glad to have me as an excuse to leave Suzy Solidors's; she didn't much like night clubs in the first place and she had had a moment of jealousy, I could see it. She was a satellite circling the sun.

Chapter 29

I walked back from school through Cagnes on my familiar route, passing the downtown café windows, glancing in at the teenage boys playing pinball, tilting and jamming the machines, past the scooters in front on the street lined in rows. I walked past the colorful displays of food in the window of the charcuterie, eyeing the meats and cheeses, thinking about dinner as I headed up the hill toward home. I climbed the steep hill into Haut de Cagnes, reveling in the beauty of the varied shades of sienna on the buildings in the winter afternoon, the sun casting shadows, and the flatness and texture of the walls, delighted by the colorful flowers in planters on painted window frames, glancing down to watch my step so as not to stumble over cobblestones.

Soon enough I snapped out of this reverie. I arrived home at my usual time, 5:00 p.m., and Lily wasn't home. I walked into the kitchen and opened the refrigerator. Nothing. There was no Lily and there was no food in Le Cave.

With the images of the charcuterie still fresh in my mind, the succulent meats and cheeses laid out in the windows, I immediately headed down to the bar Tabac to find Lily. I knew she'd be there. I walked fast, feeling hungry and irritated.

The bar was full of people drinking after work aperitifs, and Lily was in the back playing gin rummy with Kathleen and Lando. She looked up and saw me.

"Back here!" She waved at me. I made my way through the crowd to the back of the room.

"Do you want to play? You can play the next hand."

"There's no place to sit," I said, becoming uneasy. Lily was drinking pastis. "You can sit on my lap," Lando offered.

"Gin!" said Kathleen.

"No," I said.

"No, what? You don't want to play cards?" Lando said. He noticed my uneasiness, not knowing it was about Lily drinking pastis. "No, I don't want to sit on your lap."

"Too old or too young?"

"Both."

Lando looked at me thoughtfully. "I see," he said.

Lily had been listening in on the conversation and smiled slightly, not bothering to look up from her cards.

"Take my seat. I'm leaving," Lando said and stood up.

"Are you sure?"

"I'm sure," he said. He said goodbye and left.

Kathleen dealt the cards, shuffling the deck expertly, dealing me in for the next hand. She had barely glanced up from the deck.

Lily seemed distracted and kept glancing at another table. I looked over and saw a woman sitting across from us, a strikingly beautiful woman who sat with one booted leg propped on a chair, leaning back against the wall. She was sitting with a young man. She was made up and dressed in a riding jacket, tight pants, and black leather riding boots and in her hand she held a riding crop with which she swatted the side of her boot intermittently. She was watching Lily with veiled eyes.

Lily sipped her pastis and slid down in her chair, hiding her face behind her cards, and I could see her return the glances. Kathleen was paying no attention to any of this and focused on the cards. We played cards.

After a while, I said, "Mom, there's no food in the house."

"I know. I didn't go shopping," Lily replied quietly, laying two cards on the table. Kathleen dealt her new cards.

"So what are we going to do for dinner?"

"I don't know," Lily said with a curt voice. I was familiar with this tone of voice; it was the voice Lily used to curtail or end a conversation. Kathleen glanced up with owl-like eyes, peering over the top of her glasses at me.

"Do you see that woman?" Lily said.

"What woman?"

"The one with the riding crop."

I looked at the woman with the riding crop and thought she was beautiful and seemed unusual. Then I scrutinized at the woman's companion, wondering who a woman like that would be with. He was a more ordinary-looking individual than she was, yet he projected an unmistakable aura of something I couldn't quite put my finger on, eccentricity perhaps, or wealth. He was dressed in khakis and a loose-fitting corduroy jacket, and wore a hat with earflaps. He had curly, blond hair that stuck out from under the cap, a wispy beard and mustache, and wore wire-rimmed spectacles. A plaid scarf was thrown carelessly around his neck and shoulders. The woman looked at me and then at Lily, and then away.

Lily said, "Is she watching me?"

"I think she is, yes," I said.

Lily's face turned even redder than it already was, and she sunk down even further in her seat and hid her face behind the fanned out cards in her hands.

"Gin!" said Kathleen. She collected the small pot and then, after looking at Lily with a small amount of exasperation, stood up.

"That's it for me," she said. She had no patience for whatever intrigue might be taking place between Lily and this strange woman sitting across from us. She looked down at me with sympathy. I wanted it to be "it" for Lily also. I wanted to leave and go home, but Lily ordered another pastis and my heart sank.

The two of us sat at the table alone, Lily drinking her pastis and becoming more emboldened. She quit bothering to be discrete about watching the beauty at the other table. The woman whispered something to her companion and the man turned and looked at Lily. He looked cross.

"Can we go to the restaurant and eat when you're finished?" I said.

I was slumped down in my chair, thinking wistfully of the meats and cheeses in the windows of the charcuterie, and my walk home from school. Then I thought about the roast chicken that they served at the restaurant, and the first time I ate the soft, round potatoes served with chicken, and that perhaps I could have them tonight.

"We can't go there anymore. I've been 86'd."

"What do you mean?" I said with a distinct tone of alarm in my voice.

"They asked me to not come back."

"They did? Why?" My voice was suddenly louder. I'd never heard of such a thing. Not only did it mean no chicken and potatoes, which was disappointing, but it was embarrassing.

Lily's face darkened. "I got drunk in there and they asked me to not come back," she said. "We can't go there anymore."

"You better not do that here!" I said. "We won't have anywhere to go!"

"I won't. I know you're right," Lily said quietly, chagrinned. She took a tiny sip of the pastis to emphasize the point, a very tiny sip.

"Get something here," Lily said. "You can have eggs or a sandwich."

I went up to the bar and looked at a jar of eggs on the counter and wondered how long they had been floating in the greenish liquid. I ordered a sandwich.

It was getting more and more crowed in the bar, and a heavyset man came in and stood in the middle of the room. He stood at least a head taller than the other people. He lit a pipe and started to smoke and an amiable expression developed on his face, partly obscured by smoke and a shank of straight dark hair that fell over his fore-head. He was dressed in a non-descript American fashion; loose slacks, open-collared plaid shirt, and leather shoes. He was obviously American and he looked incongruous.

"Do you see that man?" Lily said.

It was difficult to miss him.

"Yeah.".

"That's Mike," she said. "I think he works for the CIA."

"He does?"

"Oh yeah."

"Is he a spy?"

Lily laughed. "Maybe. Mike!" She waved at him. "He's nice. I'll introduce you."

Mike came over and looked down at me.

"Hello, Lily," Mike said with a warm and familiar voice, as if they were old friends.

"This is my daughter, Suzanne," Lily said.

"Hi, Suzanne." He bent down to shake my hand. Then he straightened up, and standing tall lit his pipe. "Are you enjoying yourself tonight?"

"Yes."

Mike looked off into the crowd. He was a man of few words.

"Mike works at the American Embassy," Lily said.

Mike's pipe went out.

"I love the smell of that tobacco you smoke," Lily said. "What kind is it?"

Mike smiled and pulled out a packet of tobacco and said it was cherry something. Then he tapped the ash out of his pipe and packed it again and lit up. A sweet cherry tobacco smell wafted across the room.

"Doesn't that smell good?" Lily said. "Usually I don't like the smell of pipe tobacco, but that smells really good." I inhaled the sweet tobacco smell and agreed that it smelled wonderful.

It was getting late, and Lily was still nursing her pastis, the same pastis she had had for an hour. Mike wandered off leaving a clear view between the woman with the switch who was now alone, her companion having left. She returned Lily's glance and swatted her boot.

"You go on home, it's late. You have to go to school in the morning," Lily said.

"Aren't you coming?"

"I'm not ready to leave. I'll come later."

Chapter 30

Something was very wrong when I came home from school the next day. Standing on the steps of Le Cave that went down into my mother's room, the main room, I saw that Lily was in her bed in the corner, a lump under the covers. There really was no privacy in Le Cave. I was relieved to see that she was home; I hadn't seen her since I left her in the bar Tabac, but now here she was in bed at 5:00 p.m.

I shut the door softly behind me and went and stood in the middle of the room, closer to her bed. Clumps of her hair stuck out on the pillow, the only visible part of her; her face was completely hidden under blankets.

"Mom?" I said.

"I'm here," Lily said. Her voice was throaty and slurred and my heart sank. Lily raised her head up out of the covers and I could see her face. It was bad. She was totally shit-faced drunk.

"Where were you?" I said about her not coming home the previous night.

"I wazzzat . . ." Lily collapsed back down into the covers. "Oh—"

"Are you getting up?"

"Mmmm, no, Idonethinkso."

"What about dinner?"

That was wishful thinking. It was obvious she couldn't get up and cook dinner, and I didn't even know why the words came out of my mouth. It wasn't dinner I was so concerned about; what I wanted was my mother. I moved closer to her bed and looked down at her. It was a disturbing sight—a dirty glass, a half-empty liquor bottle, cigarettes, and an overflowing ash-tray of butts. Anxiety gripped me and suddenly I didn't want to be here in this place with Lily, and I felt afraid.

"Go upstairs," Lily slurred. "Noel can make you dinner."

I moved quickly away from my mother, lying in her bed of drunken stupor. I dropped my satchel in my room with a thud and went upstairs. From the porch outside, I could see Noel moving around inside the kitchen preparing a meal and I knocked on the door. Noel looked up and quickly opened the door.

"Did you see Mom?"

"I know," Noel said. "It's awful." She stood there a moment and studied my face. "It's not the first time you've seen her like that is it?"

"No."

She reached out and pulled me to her and held me close. Noel hugged me as if she wanted to fix the problem with her hug, and I hugged her back but it was a bittersweet moment. As Noel held me, I felt suddenly old for the very first time in my life. The whole situation was just too familiar, and as much as it was comforting to be hugged by Noel, or to be comforted by anyone for that matter over my mother's drunkenness, there was a familiarity to it that just didn't feel right.

Noel prepared dinner and we ate in a hushed atmosphere, as if something was an emergency. Noel was obviously shocked by Lily's behavior and wanted to discuss the why, the how often, and the what to do about it all with me, and I tried to oblige her, but the truth of it was that I didn't want to talk or even think about Lily and her drunkenness. I wanted to just enjoy my dinner with Noel. Noel soon realized this and changed the conversation, attempting to carry on the dinner with a degree of normalcy, but it was unavoidable—Lily was on our minds, as was the fact that I was going to go back downstairs to Le Cave to bed.

"Do you want to stay up here tonight?" Noel offered with a look of perplexed concern, as if she was envisioning the drunken Lily downstairs in her messy lair. I could read her mind.

"It's ok," I said. "She's probably sleeping by now." I knew my mother, and I knew she was sleeping it off. The dinner ended with another long embrace and Noel watched me leave with uncertainty in her eyes. Downstairs, Lily was snoring loudly as I noiselessly crept into my bed.

Chapter 31

January was filled with days of gray, wet weather pouring rain. I looked out my small window from the shelter of Le Cave at the rivulets of water streaming down the glass, outside the garden a green blur with gray sky behind. It felt good to be looking out from the warmth of my room, and I was excited by the storm; I could hear the thunder cracking.

"It's raining really hard!"

Lily emerged from the gloom of her room, from back in Le Cave and came up beside me. She stood next to me and looked at the water outside uneasily. We could already feel a chill dampness creeping in, seeping in through the cracks and crannies of Le Cave, under the doors and through the sills. Noel had warned Lily about living down here through the winter rains and that it flooded. Lily was the first to notice a slick of water on the recessed sill of the window.

"Water is coming in under the window," she said. "It isn't sealed."

I looked down at the water. From the wall to the windowpane it was at least a six-inch recession and a puddle had formed. The water started to run down along the side of the wall forming a damp stain on the new white paint.

"I see it!" I said. "You think more will come?"

"I don't know," Lily said. "It might. Noel said it sometimes floods down here in heavy rains."

"She said that?" I said. I didn't remember her saying that and looked at my mother in disbelief. Disbelief that we would be living here. "Can we go upstairs?"

Lily shook her head. It not an option for us to take refuge in the house upstairs. Noel was sick, and we couldn't disturb her, and Lily was still in the doghouse as a result of her drunken binge, so we could not go upstairs.

"Noel needs to be quiet and rest," Lily said.

I nodded, okay.

"I'm sorry. She told me it might be like this when we moved in," Lily said. It was obvious she felt bad about the situation. She had gotten drunk, and now she had failed in a most basic way; she hadn't provided decent shelter.

"Let's put towels down so the water won't come in," she said. She got towels and pushed them up against the bottom of the window, then we moved my bed away from wall. We went to bed that night and huddled under our covers, the rain pelting the glass, and hoped for the best. During the night, Le Cave flooded.

We woke up the next morning to bright sunshine and water everywhere in Le Cave. The walls of my room were streaked by the damp plaster, and water was pooled on the floor by my bed.

"Mom!"

"What?! What is it?" Lily had been lying in bed awake, dreading getting up.

"There's water on the floor by my bed!"

"Step around it," Lily said in a little voice.

I stretched my legs out and sat upright on the bed, then carefully stepped down avoiding a large pool of water on the floor. In the kitchen I could see water on the floor as well—it had come in under the door.

"It's in here too," Lily said.

"It is?"

Worst of all, the rain had flowed down the steps from the outside street and under the front door into Lily's room. Not only was there a large puddle at the foot of the steps, but the carpet Lily had put down was soaked.

"Yes," Lily sighed and roused herself to get up; she had to face it. "It came down from the street,"

I came in and looked around Lily's room. "Oh wow," I said. "It's in the kitchen too."

Lily sighed. "I'm sorry," she said.

"It's not your fault."

"I should have found a better place for us. For you," Lily said. She looked like she was about to cry, but she held the tears back.

"It's okay, Mom," I said. Yes, it was uncomfortable in this damp place, but the truth was I really didn't mind it so much. I had my mother back. She was sober and we were together. Lily got out of bed and got towels to sop up the water, but there wasn't much we could do about the walls. The plaster was soaked through in many spots, and it would take hours, if not days, to dry out. We did what we could.

"This place isn't really meant to be lived in," My mother said. She looked around her in distaste; Le Cave was now a damp hovel.

"I like it here," I said. I was trying to cheer her up.

"You do?" It worked.

Lily dragged the carpet out and laid it over the wall in the garden in the sun to dry. Then she came back into Le Cave.

"I'll be right back," she announced. "I'm going upstairs to talk to Noel and tell her what happened."

She had a look about her, that there was no stopping her. I watched her as she marched up the stairs, determined to set things right, if not for herself then for me. Lily's mind was made up; she had decided what to say. Whatever it was she did say, I thought, must have been very clever. I could hear Noel laughing from in front of Le Cave where I was standing in the garden.

"I warned you!" Noel said, then she stopped laughing. They reconciled, Lily and Noel, after the flood. And the warm weather held out long enough for Le Cave to dry out. Life went back to normal.

Chapter 32

Kathleen, Lily, Lando, and I were sitting at a table in the back of the Bar Tabac playing cards. I was facing the door and was the first to see her coming, Frieda was craning her neck to see over the crowd at the bar Tabac (she was quite short) and our eyes met. I could tell there was something wrong as I watched her thread her way through the crowd with a determined grim face.

She arrived at our table.

"Noel needs her medication! She's out of medication!"

The four of us looked up, and Lily and Lando gaped. Kathleen, as usual, was winning at gin rummy and looked up over her bifocals at Frieda with an expression of mild irritation. There was a pile of bills in the middle of the table.

"Why don't you go to the pharmacy and buy it?" Lily suggested calmly. She looked back at her cards and pulled a card out and placed it on the table.

"It's closed! It's Sunday!" Frieda said breathlessly. "She was on the street yelling for medication."

"She was?" Lily said. Her face became grave, and she laid her cards face down on the table, and then Lando and I laid ours down. Kathleen pulled hers closer to her chest in a firm grasp.

She told us that Noel had been out in the street in pajamas and robe, staggering and hollering for medication and that the holidays had done her in. The neighbors had been watching the spectacle out the window, but had not come out to help. I imagined them peering out of their windows, partially concealed behind transparent curtains, listening to Noel's voice subsiding from a yell into a moan and then a whimper.

"She was screaming in the middle of the street that she's in pain and that she's dying", Freida said. "She said she needs her medication …immediately."

"She was in the middle of the street!?" Lily said.

"She's back inside now. I put her to bed!" Freida quickly said."Her bed of pain."

We all stared at her. including Kathleen.

"She called it her bed of pain." Freida elaborated. Kathleen sighed loudly.

"Sit down," Kathleen said. "She's not going to die this afternoon."

Lando pulled a chair up and Frieda plunked herself down next to Lily and exhaled. Kathleen pulled her cards close to her body to hide them from Frieda's view.

"Now why would she go out on the street and yell like that?" she said in her old lady gravelly voice. "What good does she think that will do?" She practically spit these last words out.

Frieda went limp in the chair.

"She's being dramatic," Lando said, and a smile crept across his face. "Maybe she wants attention."

"Obviously she wants attention!" Lily said and I noticed a sardonic smile developing on her face. I wondered if her feelings might be hurt that Noel had called Frieda and not her, but now it seemed like they all were thinking perhaps Frieda was being played for a fool, and that now they were all being played. Frieda herself seemed to be feeling much better now and yes, looked as if she felt foolish. Nevertheless, something must be done for Noel, and these were the people to do it.

"Can you call her doctor?" Lando said.

"He won't be there on a Sunday," Kathleen rasped. "He's my doctor too. And besides, he writes the prescriptions, he doesn't have the drugs to dispense."

They mulled the situation over.

"She just needs the drugs not the doctor," Frieda said, emphasizing the point.

They mulled the situation over some more. I was unclear on how seriously to take the situation, was this drama for real or a game? Watching the faces of the adults I just couldn't tell, but I got the feeling it wasn't so serious.

"I'll get her something," Lando finally said.

"How? The pharmacy is closed."

"I have some pills at my house. I'll take them to her."

"What pills?"

"Aspirin. I'll take her some aspirin. I'll give her a placebo."

Frieda smiled. "A placebo?" she repeated.

"I won't tell her it's aspirin. I'll tell it's her medication. What is it that she takes? Codeine? She will think it's her regular pill and won't know the difference."

"I don't know . . ." Frieda said.

Lily snickered.

"I don't want to take her aspirin," Frieda said.

"Why not?" Lando said. "I am betting she won't know the difference."

Frieda didn't say anything.

"I'll take it over to her," Lando said. "I'll tell her I had some on hand from a war injury." He was a vet from the Korean War.

Kathleen laughed outright and the rest of them giggled. I was sure now that this wasn't so serious. They were going to give Noel fake medication, a placebo. "Placebo." I thought and turned the word and the idea of it over in my mind.

Lando left the bar Tabac and we started back in on our uneasy and distracted game of cards while waiting for him to come back and update us on the situation. Frieda said something about blowback from Noel and about how this was going to play out; she wasn't so sure Noel would be fooled by the fake pill and everyone nodded and said not to worry about it, because it wasn't her idea. She then quickly agreed, relaxed and took Lando's place at the table playing cards, happy to let him handle it. Forty-five minutes later Lando returned.

"It's fine," he said. His eyes were gleaming. "I gave her the pill and she went right to sleep,"

"She did?" Lily said. Frieda was silent.

"Yes." He nodded.

"What did you tell her?"

"I told her we found an open pharmacy and got her some pills."

"She believed you?"

"I think so."

Kathleen and Lily shook their heads. I could tell Lily was glad that she hadn't been the one Noel called. Then they all laughed and I laughed along with them. The crisis was over.

Chapter 33

Noel had a sly look on her face, as if she had something up her sleeve. She was sitting with Lily in her living room when I came home from school. I came upstairs from Le Cave looking for Lily and immediately knew something was up. It was the day after the episode in the street and the fake pill and Noel was up and feeling better but still looking pale. I put my satchel on the floor and sat down with them.

"They're in her studio. I know where she would put them," Noel said to no one in particular.

"What's in her studio?" I said.

"Noel's medicine is in Frieda's studio," Lily explained. "Frieda got it, but it's in her studio." Frieda had been to the pharmacy and bought Noel's medication.

"She needs to get it," Lily said. Lily looked contrite; she was still in the doghouse. Then she smiled like a cat that had just eaten a mouse.

"Where's Frieda?" I said. Something was definitely up.

"Oh, she had to go into town for some business," Noel said. "Her Visa ran out. She had to go to the embassy."

"What does that mean?"

"Never mind that," Noel said.

"She has to get her visa renewed," Lily said, "and Noel needs her medication now."

Noel eyed me. "I have the key to her studio."

"So why don't you go and get it?" I said. "If you have the key—"

"Oh no, I can't," Noel said. "I'm not allowed to go into her studio."

Lily giggled.

"Why not?"

"She's doing a sculpture of Noel and she doesn't want her to see it until it's finished," Lily explained.

"She is?!" I said.

Noel nodded.

"I commissioned a sculpture," Noel said.

"What's a commission?"

"She's paying Frieda to do a sculpture of her head and bust," Lily said. "That's what a commission is."

"I want to know how far along she is," Noel said. "If she's done anything!"

I looked at Noel and smiled, thinking that she had generous heart.

"Will you go?" Noel said.

"I don't know—you could go," I said to Lily.

"Oh no. I'm not going in her studio without her there," Lily shook her head firmly.

"I need my medicine and Frieda likes you," Noel said. "If anyone should go it's you. She won't get mad at you."

I knew that this was true. "Okay," I said. "I'll go."

"I want to know how it's coming along," Noel said. "Check and see how the sculpture is coming along."

"What do you mean?"

"See how far she's gotten."

"Okay." I took the key and left with a sense of purpose. I was on a secret mission.

When I walked into Frieda's studio I stopped just side of the door and immediately my spirits lifted. I hadn't even been aware of the heaviness of spirit I'd been feeling about Noel being sick and my uncertainty about life with Lily. I looked around. Shafts of light slanted in through the windows, and artist's tools lay about among dust and clay. For moments I stood looking at the clay figurines and the stone heads, clay twisted into female forms attached to wires on stands, and the heads sitting in the corners. It was a world of creation. The regular implements of living were hardly noticeable; they were off to the side like an afterthought, a bed made up into a couch, and a small kitchen with a few utensils. I smiled. A head was in the center of the room on a stand surrounded by a circle of dust and a cloth was draped over it. I could tell from the shape under the cloth, and from the drape of the covering, what it was. I moved through the room, my eyes sliding over clay figurines lining the shelves as I passed, graceful female forms bent into positions of dance and bowing down or reaching out.

Small chisels and hammers lay on a table next to the bust, and when I reached it in the center of the room, I stood in front of the bust, I picked up a small chisel off the table and turned it over on my palm, wondering at the exact magnitude of the tool. Then I took the cloth off the bust.

It was Noel, in all her insouciance, with her nose upturned slightly, sculpted in marble, more than a perfect likeness carved out of the hard, smooth stone. The sculpture graced the room and completely filled it. It was magnificent. I stood and looked at it and then down at the chisel, marveling at the skill it must require to produce something like this out of this hard stone from this tool in my hand. I reached out and caressed the smoothness of the stone, marveling even more. Suddenly I felt as if I was intruding on something private. It was too beautiful for me to have even imagined and the sanctity of this place should be respected.

I quickly put the cloth back on the bust and the chisel on the table and went to find the medicines. There they were, right where Noel had said they would be in a drawer in the kitchen. I grabbed them and with a last look at the shelves lined with figurines, I noticed another beautiful head next to the door on my way out of the studio.

I hurried back to Noel and Lily, and I could hardly wait to tell them.

"It's beautiful!"

Lily's face reddened a little, as if she was almost jealous. "It is?" Lily said, like she didn't want to believe it.

"Oh yes, it's beautiful."

"I knew it," she said. "I knew she was talented . . ."

"How far along is it?" Noel said.

"It's almost finished," I said and Noel smiled, satisfied.

Chapter 34

Lily still had amends to make as a result of her binge. She had yet to get herself back in favor with me and with Noel, and she had yet to set things right. It wasn't over. The next several weeks was a period of extreme compliance on Lily's part, a period of diminishing contriteness, and it was during this interlude that I got possession of the Vespa.

She was having a difficult time with the machine anyway. My mother, who was raised on a farm and a woman who was handy with a hacksaw and hammer, a woman who could build a fence and capable of bad yet practical carpentry, was something of a mechanical idiot. She was incompetent at the simplest of mechanical tasks, such as fastening a seatbelt. Often, after a few futile attempts at some simple thing, like say pushing the lever of a car seat down to adjust the seat, she would simply give up in frustration. The task at hand just wouldn't get done unless there was someone there to do it for her.

The Vespa turned out to be too much of a challenge for her. To start it you had to gas it by turning the handle and kick-start it simultaneously. She just couldn't get the hang of it, even after repeated explanations and demonstrations. And when it came to a stop and idled, the Vespa needed to be gassed, just a little, and Lily couldn't grasp this either. She ended up stranded at various locations after the engine died and then couldn't start it back up. She could start it up only by accident, after turning and twisting the handles and kicking and cursing for several minutes. As expected, this didn't always work.

On the other hand, I got the knack of the machine after a couple of tries. It was really simple. I explained to Lily, "You need to twist the knob and gas it. No problem."

"Mmmhm," Lily said with her mouth pursed.

I got the keys on a day not too long after the drunken debacle. Lily abandoned the scooter down the street from Le Cave, right in front of Tony's doorstep, and walked up the hill the rest of the way. She asked me if I could go down and start it, and told me I could keep the keys if I could get it back to the house

"I can ride it whenever I want?" I said, hearing my voice sound squeaky. I felt exultant. I loved to ride the Vespa; it was absolutely one of the most fun things in the world to do.

"Yes," Lily said. "Just don't ride it down in the town."

She still had that abashed contrite look on her face, the after-the-drunken-binge look. She was still trying to get back into my good graces.

"Okay," I quickly agreed. This was a *coup de grace*.

"I can't ride that damn thing anyway," Lily said. We were both smiling now.

Chapter 35

I was flying through a beautiful place in this world. Helmetless, the wind whipped my hair back from my face, and the warmth of the sun fell across my face. I felt the wind and sun on my face and the thrum and vibration of the Vespa underneath me and through my body. I was on the windy road behind Haut de Cagnes riding through carnation fields. Rows of colorful flowers looped up and over and around the hillsides, the landscape broken up by large and grandiose oaks standing in dominion over the fields, branches opening up and sheltering seeming to greet me with a welcoming "Allo!" It was delightful to ride the Vespa in this place behind the town in the rolling hills and smell the fragrance of the breeze in the warmth of the winter sun. I was in the world, and everything felt right in my world. There was no future or past for me, but just the of sensations of riding the scooter and the sweetness in the air and my appreciation of the beauty surrounding me. I rode a long ways along a ridge behind the town until I came to a stop at a crossroads.

A sign read "Vence, 10 Kilometers."

I felt a stab of nervousness knowing I had gone really far. I was a kid who was far away from home. The scooter was sputtering, and I turned it around to go back, but the engine died. I sat there in the middle of the deserted road listening to the silence of the place, and then a bee hummed and circled around me and a bird darted and twittered out of the branches of an oak. There was an old stone farmhouse down a rutted dirt road nearby, and I sat on the Vespa looking at it for moments. I swatted at the bee and wondered vaguely who might have lived there for the past hundred years, thinking how things in this place were measured in centuries, in hundreds of years. There was no movement around the old stone house, but it looked lived in. It was at least a hundred years old, maybe a thousand, who knew? Not me. Then I started up the Vespa and headed back down the road toward home.

Chapter 36

Lando had finished a series. He had come up with an "idea" and was going to give a presentation of his works and his "idea." He invited Noel, who invited Lily, who invited me to his studio. We were to be the first to see these new works (other than his lover, a local Frenchwoman), and be witness to his brainstorm.

Noel's feelings about this event were revealed in the snarky way she announced the preview to us, Lily and me.

"Do you want to go to Lando's studio?" She said breezily. "He has some new idea he's all excited about that he wants to show us."

"He wants to show us his paintings?" Lily said. She was thrilled, impressed that he had a body of work to show, and I caught her feeling of excitement. Yes! I wanted to go see Lando's paintings, we had been curious for so long—it was an event!

"He's going to show us his paintings, but he has another idea he's excited about. Something else he wants to show us."

"What?"

"I have no idea," Noel said. "We have to go over there to find out."

There was something about the look on Noel's face—a blank expression and veiling in her eyes that betrayed her, like she was trying to hide a feeling of contempt, albeit affectionate contempt. It was the look an older sister might have for a little brother that she loved but who just shit his pants. It was a signal to not take this presentation too seriously but to go through the motions and be present out of politeness. It was already established in Noel's opinion that Lando was not a good artist and nothing could change this fact, certainly not any new "idea" he might have.

Nevertheless, Lily and I didn't have any opinion about this. Our minds were open, and we were excited about seeing his work and visiting his studio. We had never seen his paintings and had never seen his studio. We ran into him at the bar Tabac and his excitement about the presentation was infectious.

"Noel asked us to come to your studio," Lily said.

"You're coming with Noel?" he said.

"Yes."

"She is coming?"

"Yes," Lily nodded.

Noel was coming! She was going to give her opinion, an opinion he revered.

Lando lived in an "artist" garret on the other side of the village from us, and the whole thing was somewhat of a cliché. The garret, Lando's appearance, actually, in retrospect the whole way he was living his life. It was like he was living a fantasy of what he thought it was to be an artist in France at the turn of the century. Of course, Lily and I saw the appeal in this. Lily was in love with the French art of that period, impressionism, and we both could understand and admire Lando in this pursuit. Noel on the other hand saw it as artificial and his work as unoriginal.

At any rate, the three of us walked through the village to his house in high spirits. He was in a state of nervous agitation when we arrived, and had cleaned his studio and prepared for the presentation. He ushered us into his garret, a room with a sloping attic ceiling in which you had to duck. It was full of art. His girlfriend, who spoke not a word of English, was seated on a built-in bed, smiling cat-like and happy, sipping wine.

Lily and I started to look at the paintings, but he told us to wait, so we stood still in the middle of the room and waited. Then he pulled a cloth away from a painted pane of glass that was backlit by a lamp.

"This is it!" he announced, his eyes shining.

"What?" Lily said. She was puzzled.

Noel and I stood there looking the glass painting.

"I'm going to paint my paintings on glass and light them from behind!"

Lily nodded. Then she said, "Why? What's the matter with the ones on the canvas?" She edged away and looked at a canvas leaning against wall, then flicked it back to see the one behind it.

"I like these," she said. Lando's lover smiled even more, and she sipped more wine.

Lando looked a bit impatient.

"I can't get a show with those paintings," he said brusquely.

"You can't? I like them," Lily said, sounding vague. I noticed a distinct smirk on Noel's face.

"But with this," Lando said, standing by the glass painting lit by the lamp. "I think I can get a show with this idea. I'll have a series of these, all lit from behind."

Lily came back over and stood in front of it.

"So what do you think?" Lando said. He stood there with his arm stretched out pointing toward the painted glass. He waited for her response. She looked at him and then at back at the painting for moments. I stood there with her.

"It's beautiful," Lily said.

Lando nodded and smiled slightly, like he didn't believe her.

"I like it," I said. The painting was a small painting of Haut de Cagnes, the buildings delineated by blocks of paint done with a palette knife.

Noel was standing behind us silently watching.

He turned to her. "What do you think?" he said.

"I don't know, Lando . . ." she hedged, trying to be diplomatic. He had an eager boyish look on his face. "How would they even hang them in a gallery?" she said.

This caught him by surprise and he had to think about it.

"They could hang them in little alcoves," he finally said. "With the lights behind." Clearly he was flummoxed by the question. The mechanics of hanging them was something he had taken for granted; the gallery could take care of it. He hadn't considered that this might be a problem. But now the thought on all our minds was, "How many galleries in Paris have little alcoves?" As he stood there, his arm dropped to his side and he looked grave.

Noel moved away from the glass painting and started looking around at his other canvases.

"Do you have any new work? Show me," she said.

"Yes," Lando said. "Those are new, right there," he sounded utterly unenthusiastic. In fact, he looked pale and suddenly drained. He watched bleakly as Noel rifled through a stack of canvases that were leaning against the wall, looking at each of them briefly, spending just seconds on each individual painting. Lando's lover, still on the couch with her wine, looked grave.

"You're getting better," Noel said.

Lily and I stood in the middle of the room and watching.

"You think so?" Lando said. Hope crossed his face.

"Yes," Noel said as she straightened up. "These are definitely better."

Lando looked eager.

"I think you should concentrate on these and keep working at it. Don't worry about getting a show in Paris. You're improving.," Noel said. "Don't use gimmicks."

"You think painting on glass is a gimmick?"

"Yes."

Lando was crestfallen. His lover put down the wine and looked down at her hands, limp in her lap. A hush fell over the garret. The presentation was over, and Lando showed us the door.

Noel was irritated as we walked down the street. "I don't know why he would even come up with that idea. It's a gimmick."

"I thought it was beautiful," Lily said.

"They won't give him a show in Paris with that!" Noel said, practically spitting the words out. She cast a dark look at Lily.

"Mmmm," Lily said. She wasn't quite back into Noel's good graces after the debauch, so she didn't disagree.

I walked along and kept silent, thinking about Lando and his studio, about the back-lit painting and how excited he had been to show them, and about his French girlfriend, and how she couldn't speak English. I felt a little sorry for Lando; it was obvious that things weren't going so well. He couldn't get a show in Paris, and this was something he seemed to want and need.

Chapter 37

There was an overall shabbiness about the place; the dirty walls with bare patches and peeling paint, the windowsills nicked and splintered and worn into grooves, and the footpaths ruts, but nevertheless something about the stable pulled me in. It was the riding ring. There was a solid wall built around the ring, sheets of wood nailed together that slanted slightly outward and upward, creating a bowl-like effect, and this was unusual in itself. But it was the sea on the other side of the wall that captured my mind. I had the idea that I would have a view of the sea while riding in this ring. I wanted to ride there so I could look out at the water as I rode around.

I was looking for a new stable having quit the old one. They hadn't advanced me to the next level along with the rest of the group, and this blow to my pride was unacceptable. I was ready to move on without looking back.

I had passed this particular stable, the one with the ring by the sea many times; it was located at the junction of the roads.

"What about that place?" I had said on my last trip by to the old stable. I was with Noel and

Lily, who was making the trip in a last ditch effort set things right. I knew better, and was marveling at how blue the sea was, and how enticing it looked past the wall of the riding ring at this "other" stable.

"It's not a good stable," Noel said. She glanced over her shoulder at me. "They don't keep it up."

I craned my neck to look at the horses. There was a group in the ring circling around, and then I looked past them at the blue water. It looked good.

"The horses look okay," I said.

"You won't like it," Noel said.

"I want to try it," I said.

Lily, sitting next to Noel in the front seat, turned around and smiled at me. "Let her try it," she said.

"Okay, okay," Noel said.

Me and my horse trotted around the ring with a herd of horses and riders. From one side of the ring I could see a small portion of water, just a small section of blue over the top of the wall across the roadway that ran between the stable and the sea. The horse fell into a familiar groove, a jarring trot circling the ring, and seemed unsettled. It was crowded, and the horse seemed to be waiting for an opening to break away from the circling and make her way back to her stable, or maybe she had something more wild in mind. It was hard to tell, but I had to pay attention and keep her reined in.

I quit trying to look over the wall and focused on holding the horse in and also on the hooves of the horses in front of us, on avoiding them. The horse seemed to want to run into the horse just ahead, like she had no sense at all. At the end of the ring, at the turn I noticed ridges of dirt building up against the wall. The ring hadn't been raked, and we were trotting in a gutter of soil. Not particularly liking this view, I made an another effort to look out over the wall at the sea, but my horse pressed ahead faster into an even more jangling and more jarring trot, so I turned my attention back to the press of horses. My eyes fell on the same spot of dirt and wall every time we went around the curve, going back to this same spot of ridges of dirt building up against the wall as we passed, curious to see how high it go, mesmerized by how it slid down just a little as it built up.

Then I looked up and I noticed dirt flying off the hooves of the horses up against the wall and slip down the wood, leaving brown clots stuck in the small crevices and splinters. I thought of the sheer number of riders and horses that had trotted around in this circular rut, the incredible volume. Why, there must have been hundreds, if not thousands, over the years flinging bits of dirt against the wall . . . a vague and fleeting feeling of the being stuck in an endless and useless exercise of trotting around in circles overcame me, and I felt a sudden rush of empathy with my horse. When we rounded the ring yet again, I raised my eyes up from where the dirt met the wall to the spots of flecks of soil slowly falling and creating small piles down below. It was clear now, the grime of this place, and the fatigue of the horses and the looming resignation of my horse. This was why the horse wanted to break away, and I knew I couldn't help the horse break away—I was part of the problem. I wanted to leave.

I understand, I thought to the horse, as I pet her and put her away. The horse snorted sadly and looked into my eyes, wanting to understand why she had to endure this drudgery and we parted.

"You were right," I said to Noel on the ride home. I felt badly about the horse.

"I told you," Noel said.

Chapter 38

I was loping around the carefully combed riding ring on a spirited bay. I was feeling grand and vindicated. I had found a new stable and the disappointing experience at the old one was just an unpleasant memory of no consequence at all.

I was the lone rider in the class and the center of attention. The riding master stood in the middle of the ring swatting his crop against his jodhpurs and focused his attention solely on me. The horse loped around the edge of the ring, warming up before starting in on the course, a long and formidable series of jumps. This wasn't my first time out on the course, but I was still new to it.

The riding master was impeccably dressed in a clean, white shirt, pressed jodhpurs, and high black boots with brown around the top. His handsome, leathery face was clean-shaven, and his head of graying hair was neatly combed and gelled off his forehead. His manner was polite as to the point of obsequiousness, and I didn't mind this at all.

It was a beautiful setting. The ring was carefully groomed, and a thicket of fragrant Eucalyptus trees ran along one side of the fence swaying in the breeze. The clean and freshly painted stables lay up a short incline, and happy horses hung their handsome heads over the top of their stable doors and rustled on freshly laid straw. I inhaled the sweet, fresh air and the fragrance of the Eucalyptus as I loped the horse slowly round the ring, taking it all in.

I, of course, was dressed in my riding gear, and thought about how my boots matched the instructors. I thought about London and the day my mother and I went shopping at Harrods, and that it was late afternoon by the time we had found the store that sold riding gear. The room was a large and open space, with tables piled with clothes, and sunlight fell through the windows in shafts of light. It had been the same time of day as now, with me loping around the ring. The store and the room had seemed musty to me—the clothes gave it this feeling, worsted wool riding jackets and jodhpurs, plaid cardigans and caps with earflaps. Hats I had never seen before and laughed at while trying them on—these clothes were so old-fashioned, I thought.

"They are classics," Lily had said. "They never go out of style." My mother had become extremely demure in her interaction with the well-groomed solicitous sales clerk, projecting an aura of sophistication and wealth as she bought me the wool riding jacket and high black leather riding boots, and I didn't conceal my delight. They reminded me of the steeple chasers we'd seen in the paintings at the National Gallery the day before. The boots were the kind that the steeplechasers wore, high boots of soft, black leather with a brown ring around the top. The very same boots the new riding master wore. I had thought perhaps that I would be going fox hunting, or in the very least I'd be jumping horses somewhere in this outfit, properly dressed, and here I was!

We got onto a groove as we circled the ring, the horse and me. A familiar feeling overcame me as I rode and my senses sharpened. I became a part of what was around me. I was part of the landscape, and at one with the trees, and with the horse, and with the riding ring itself, as thoughts of London drifted in and out, and the jumps were at the edge of my vision, and the landscape blurred into a passing pastiche of flashing greenery and fences, and horses' heads hanging over stable doors, and clouds and the sky, and the riding master in the center calling out some words, his crop switching rhythmically against his boot . . . boots like mine.

In an easy cantering gate, the horse and I turned and faced the first hurdle, a high jump, and the Bay snorted. I hesitated, realizing that we were coming into the jump at a slight angle and thought the jump was too high. The horse sensed my hesitation and also hesitated.

"Take the jump," I heard a voice urging us on ,and I looked from the jump up to the sky, and was thinking what a wonderful day it was, so clear and how slowly the clouds were drifting, that so much was possible in this world, and yes we could take this jump. The riding master looked up the sky at just the same time that the horse lifted up off the ground, and a black bird squawked, a cawing crow, and then the Bay's left hoof clipped the top of the jump and the horse flipped over. I tumbled off, falling clear of the somersaulting horse, who went over the jump head over hooves but avoided rolling onto me and tumbled head-first myself, landing on my riding helmet, feet loose of the stirrups, then onto my back. I lay stunned splayed out on the ground. The horse wrenched herself up off the ground with a leap, snorting wildly and trotted away fast. The riding master rushed over to me.

"Are you all right? Are you all right?"

He knelt down and peered at me as I lay dazed, looking up at the same drifting clouds. They'd moved a bit of distance I noticed. I sat up and brushed myself off.

"Yes, I'm all right."

I stood up shakily after a few moments and looked around for the horse. I'd seen her rise up from her fall with a squealing grunt. The horse was now trotting back and forth in a fast, jangling gait at the edge of the fence, snorting and snuffling and foaming at the mouth. She wanted to get out of the ring and run away. For a moment she looked over at me and I met her wary eyes, as if I'd tried to do her harm.

"The horse . . ." I said.

"Don't worry about the horse!"

I could see the white of the horse's eyes from where we stood. *The fall was my fault,* I thought, and I should have known not to take her into the jump at an angle.

"She's okay?"

"Don't worry about the horse! I'm just glad you're all right."

Chapter 39

It wasn't so much the fall from the horse (and I never went back there again), and it wasn't the flood in Le Cave, and it wasn't even that Lily was running out of money—she could have gotten a job nearby—that brought about the decision. We were in the yard outside Le Cave, less than a week after the flood, sitting in the sun.

"Do you miss your father?"

"Yes." I knew something was up. Why was she asking?

"And your brother. Do you miss John?"

"Yes, I miss him."

The truth was missing John was more a concept, rather than being an actual emotion, I had already missed him before I left. I thought about how we had grown apart.

"Do you want to go home?" my mother said.

We were in the garden in Haut de Cagnes and the sun was out. I nodded, knowing it wasn't that I missed my father or my brother, but that it was the drunken debacle. It occurred to me right then that that was why John didn't come in the first place.

My mother and I had entered that space in time between when everything was new and then it became less new, but it wasn't old yet. Since I was young, this feeling was also new, and I accepted it without question, but for my mother it was different. For her it was a signal to leave, to change her environment so as to avoid disappointment. That way she could avoid any potential dreariness or drudgery. When you were living an enchanted life, such as the life we were leading in Haut de Cages, perhaps it was better to just leave and keep it as a memory rather than let it slip into familiarity.

For me, staying would have just been a new way to be in the same place, something with the potential to be even richer in the long run. It was true that now when I walked home from school the color of the sienna village walls were no longer so rich in hue and noticeable, and it wasn't that they were fading, it just that I no longer looked as I walked up the hill at lunch time for my mid-day break. I had other things on my mind. I was thinking about picking up a couple of beers at the bar Tabac to take home and have with my lunch, a habit I had recently picked up.

Back at school, Marcie noticed the smell of the alcohol on me and I distinctly heard her emit a sigh, more than once, perhaps in resignation at her destiny. It was unfortunate. She had switched seats with a smelly, dirty girl to one who smelled like beer. The teacher also noticed my overwhelming drowsiness in the afternoon—I saw the frown—but her lectures were an intelligible drone and it was difficult to stay awake. My eyelids would flutter shut, and I'd jerk awake at Marcie's prodding elbow and see the disapproving frown on her face as well.

We won't be friends so much longer, I realized at some point, *we don't have a lot in common anyway.* A person needed to find the right place and people and it took time before that happened in a new school. It was time to make the change to be where I belonged and to be with the people I belonged with, whether I stayed in France or left.

As for Lily, I think she felt the same way that I did, that the faces of the "characters" in the village were becoming increasingly unattractive in their familiarity and their quirks and foibles becoming more like annoying weaknesses. That Le Cave after the flood was just cave-like and dark and dank, and living there was not a wonderful adventure. I had seen these things all along and accepted them, but my mother had been looking the other way and ignoring things, and that was the difference between us—the adult and the adolescent. I didn't have to sugarcoat things.

Lily couldn't abide with this. The unwelcome idea that life in France could become like a re-run, that life here could perhaps become just ordinary, was unacceptable. She seemed unwilling to stay and find out if this would happen, as if the very notion startled her, that it was a cue to leave.

"Do you want to go home?" Lily said.

I frowned. The look on my mother's face was almost anguish.

"I'm almost out of money."

I nodded. That was what it was.

"There's a job I could take nearby. We could stay. Do you want to stay?"

"I want to go home," I said. "I miss Dad." I didn't want to be alone in Le Cave with a drunken Lily again, and as much as I loved France, I was being practical. I couldn't trust that I would be taken care of by a person with cancer upstairs, Noel, as much as I cared for her, and a drunken mother downstairs. I didn't feel safe.

Chapter 40

It was a sad day when we left, bittersweet that our life in France would be over, but at the same time I was eager to get home and worried about Siggy. Noel had somewhat heartlessly (I thought) refused to commit herself to taking care of Siggy and had just shrugged her shoulders about the cat's fate. She was going to put the cat out on the street.

"She'll be a street cat," she said.

"No!"

"She can catch rats," Noel had a canny look on her face when she said this, not hard but like a street kid.

I left a pile of canned food for her in Le Cave stacked in a pyramid.

"You'll feed her the food?"

"Yeah . . ." Noel said, her eyes veiled, maybe she was lying.

It was bright and sunny the day we left, and the sea was calm and brilliant blue. There was a stillness that was similar to the day we arrived, the day we stood by the sea and got out bearings, and then looked up and to see Haut de Cagnes for the first time off in the distance.

For our journey home, Lily booked us on an Italian Ocean liner to New York. The ship was anchored far out in the harbor at Antibes and we had to take a small boat out to board. This was a fun and distracting adventure and that as well as the breathtaking beauty of the harbor in Antibes dispelled most of my sadness about leaving, but it was worse for Lily and just sad for Noel.

Noel saw us off. She stood on the dock watching our colorful, little boat puttering out through the harbor to the ship, waving all the while and I waved back and then stopped waving before she stopped waving. We were sitting upright in the little boat, Lily and I, becoming smaller and smaller from the land and from Noel. I stopped waving and just stared at the coastline of the Cote d'Azur, struck by the beauty of the sea and of Antibes and Lily started to cry. She wiped her eyes dry when the skipper of the boat glanced over. He looked away and then out to sea solemnly.

Noel finally stopped waving and turned and left the dock.

We were assigned a small cabin with two bunks, and I took the top, where I could see through a small porthole. We were situated right at the ocean's edge, and it was quite something to see the ocean water splash against the thick glass.

The ship was luxurious. It was a cruise ship and had all the amenities that cruise ships had in those days—a lounge with stylish, black leather seats (Lily found this right away since it had a bar), a kid's playroom that as it turned out was empty and unused, and an on-deck a swimming pool surrounded by lounge chairs. The water in the pool was low and surrounded by a large formidable lip. I stood on the deck and studied it, looking down at the water and wondering if it was feasible for me to swim in it. It seemed to me that it would difficult, if not impossible, to get out.

"Why is the water so far down from the edge?"

"That's so it won't splash over the side," Lily said. "We're on a ship, the boat rocks."

"Oh."

It went un-used; it was too cold to swim.

We found out right away that the main event on the ship was eating. Every day for breakfast lunch and dinner, minus a few skipped breakfasts, we trooped down and took our spots at our table. The ship's "guests" were assigned a place at a table where we sat for the duration of the trip. This arrangement had its advantages; the passengers got to know one another but boundaries of etiquette and of conversation had to be respected. We were going to be sitting with these people for the duration of the trip, and it was best to maintain a somewhat superficial conviviality but not be too overly familiar.

"What a bore," I heard Lily mutter our second day aboard. We were at the dinner table with our new companions.

I glanced at a middle-aged, overweight Englishman who somehow in some way had offended her. He looked up, startled. He had a way of talking too long and dominating the conversation, and tossing in insulting pronouncements about women in the course of his dialogues, while watching Lily with an amused glint in his eye. He was used to getting away with it.

The dining room was elegant, with tables laid out with silver and white linen and the five-course meals were served by ingratiating waiters dressed in white coats and bow ties. I could stand the bore without any problem; in fact, I didn't even know what a bore was, or why Lily called him that, but he changed tables after that night. Our table was happy he left.

Looking out across rough water from the deck, feeling the spray and the taste the salty water in cold wind, I was standing close to the bow of the ship watching a smaller ship, something that looked very old, like out of the 17th Century, a wooden ship with tall masts, rolled-up sails, bobbing up and down crazily on the rough seas.

"Look!" I shouted over the wind. I pointed at the ship to my mother, who was standing there next to me.

"It must be from Africa," Lily said.

"It looks so old."

It was a beautiful ship, but I got slightly nauseated just looking at it. It was rolling back and forth violently in the swells, herky-jerky-like.

"I'm glad I'm not on it," I said. We were still on the Mediterranean, and the weather was getting bad.

It got even rougher after we passed through the strait of Gibraltar and into the open ocean. People started throwing up all over the place, or so it seemed, and everywhere I went on the ship smelled like vomit. Lily bought some Drama-mine for us, and we were okay, but it seemed that most of the other people just suffered and were sick. The lunches and dinners went on as usual in the dining room, but the people sitting at the tables thinned out considerably.

Lily brought me into the lounge, a large room with low-slung black leather furniture and polished wood and brass tables. The staff informed her I wasn't allowed. Startled, we got up and left. We weren't in France any longer, where I could sit with my mother in the bar Tabac.

This cut into her drinking time in the bar. She not only had to babysit me, but a woman alone in a bar on an Italian ship in 1967 was . . . well, asking for it. She found this out one night when she went drinking alone and returned to the cabin with a young Italian in tow. He had walked her back to her room and followed her inside the cabin. It was a rude awakening for him to see me there. He wasn't expecting it. Neither was I. I woke up and propped myself up on one elbow to see what was going on.

"Mom?"

"Hi . . ." Lily was drunk, her words were slurred.

I was in the top bunk and looked directly into the Italian's red-rimmed brown eyes, and he looked back at me and mumbled hello. He was young and pimply, in his twenties or early thirties, and wearing tight clothes. It soon became apparent that he had one thing on his mind and was willing to pursue it, no matter whether I was there or not. He pressed against my mother and attempted to kiss her while I was still watching.

Lily pushed him away.

"Can't you see I have a daughter?" she said indignantly.

She was angry now, and he backed off, looking like a puppy dog that had been swatted. Lily quickly took advantage of the space between them and opened the cabin door wide. She pushed him toward it while talking fast.

"We can't... not with my daughter... yes... thank you, goodnight." Being diplomatic, nudging him out, she shut the door firmly behind him and locked it. Relieved, I collapsed down on the bed and covered my face with my arm.

"I'm sorry."

"Who was that guy?"

"Oh, he was just someone I met at the bar. We had a few drinks together," Lily said. "He offered to walk me back to the cabin, I didn't think he try that!"

"Oh."

Lily refrained from going back to the lounge after that night, but we were almost to New York anyway.

Chapter 41

We picked Noel up in the early evening, arriving at the airport in time for my mother to have a drink in the dome, the bar inside that iconic LA land mark that squats egg like at LAX. I didn't mind; I liked to sit in the lounge and people-watch.

I could tell Lily was nervous; she downed two cocktails before we headed to the arrival area. There were no security checkpoints, and it was just a matter of walking right up to the boarding area.

"She's in a wheelchair," I heard Lily mutter. She sounded grave.

"She is?" I said. I sounded plaintive.

We watched a uniformed attendant wheel Noel off the boarding ramp and into the boarding area. Noel spied us and gaily waved and we waved back. Then she bounded up out of the chair and the attendant stood there looking surprised as she joined us laughing. We all hugged.

"It was a ruse," Noel explained.

She did it to get the special attention, Noel said. She didn't really need to be in a wheelchair, she said and Lily nervously laughed. Laughing and feeling merry and happy to be re-united now we walked away, albeit with an undercurrent of strain on Lily's part. I couldn't help but notice the pointed look from Noel, she was assessing Lily's reaction to the wheelchair, or maybe it was the smell of alcohol on my mother's breath.

Everything was different now, I knew right away, with Noel in America.

We took her to Thai restaurant in Santa Monica and had chicken with peanut sauce.

"Do you like it?" I said.

"Yes."

"Have you had it before?"

"Yes," Noel smiled and nodded at me. Of course she had had it before, I realized, Noel was a woman of the world, a sophisticate. She looked frail, I thought, thinner and pale, but her eyes were shining. She gradually turned her attention away from me to Lily, who had been somewhat quiet and reserved, observing and listening to us talking. It was then that I saw something that I had never noticed before, something between them I was not a part of and was remote and a little repugnant to me. I became aware of a subtle power shift. Noel was on Lily's home turf, our home turf, and I noticed a look on my mother's face I hadn't seen before, the look of a fat cat who had just eaten a mouse. Turning my attention to Noel, I saw on her face was an expression of eager hope and my estimation of Noel plummeted at that moment as the two of them sat silently looking at one another. I wanted nothing to do with any of it. I knew it would come to a bad end.

Still, I was glad to see Noel.

Chapter 41

There was something incongruous about
Noel, about the way she looked sitting on the
orange sofa in front of the plate-glass windows
in the house in Malibu Canyon. The house was
1960s California modern with three walls of
floor-to-ceiling windows overlooking Malibu
Creek, and the Saddle Peak Mountains jutting up
in the distance. I liked to sit in that very spot
where Noel now sat and watch the fog roll in
over the Santa Monica Mountains. Now here
Noel was, sitting on the burnt-orange modern
sofa, in front of the windows, bent forward in an
eager posture.

Maybe it was because Noel was sitting in
"our" house, the house where I grew up with my
mother and my father, or maybe it was the
modernism of the house and the furniture and the
juxtaposition of having known Noel in the setting of a medieval French village. Whatever it
was, her sitting there in front the wall of windows and on that sofa just seemed incongruous.
Pale and thin, she seemed entirely out of place.

I looked past her and thought about the fog
rolling in over the top of the mountains; it was a

beautiful sight when it came in over the ridge like a soft ocean wave, moving slowly inland from Malibu Beach. It was clear that day, and there wasn't any fog, and Noel didn't belong in this picture—she belonged in France—but here she was in front of me, leaning forward with an earnest expression on her face.

"Do you want to talk?" she said.

This sounded serious.

"About what?"

Noel was silent a moment and looked at me with a coy expression. I found it annoying.

"You know we're homosexuals," she announced.

The way it came out, in her clipped English accent, sounded brittle and matter of fact. She was following through on a difficult decision to bring it out in the open, to lay things out on the table. I remembered then that my mother had discretely disappeared into the other room and shut the door behind her right before Noel came and sat down with me. This conversation had been planned.

"Oh, I know Mom is, but I didn't think you were," I said, sounding off hand. I didn't like where this was going.

"Oh, come on," Noel said with more than a trace of impatience. "You knew she was, but you didn't think I was, of course I am. That's ridiculous."

"Oh. I just didn't think you were." I felt embarrassed. I thought about seeing the young Frenchman in the nightclub pick Noel up and twirl her around on New Year's Eve in France and Noel laughing. She had sounded so delighted and happy in his arms at that moment that I thought she liked men. Now I just felt foolish, it was obvious I didn't understand at all.

"Well, I am," Noel said. She was perched on the edge of her seat, her hands folded in her lap and watching me, waiting for a reaction.

I didn't really care to much either way. I thought it was probably better to be heterosexual since most of the world was, but people were what they were.

"Have you always been?" I finally said, after a pause. Noel seemed to expect me to say something. "Have you ever been married?" I added.

"No, I haven't ever been married. I dated men when I was younger before I realized I was lesbian."

I could tell it was hard for her to say that last word. She averted her face from me before saying it; the conversation had become more difficult for her.

"How do you feel about it?" Noel said.

"About what?" I said absently. I was imagining Noel in her youth in a faraway land called Ireland, dating men and then deciding she was lesbian. Then I thought about Noel and foxhunting in Ireland and the horse she must have ridden. I imagined it was brownish-red with a black mane and tail and well-groomed and shiny . . .

"About this! What do you think?"

"Oh! I don't care about it," I said and quickly put the images of the young Noel and her horse out of my mind. "It doesn't bother me."

"It doesn't bother you?" Noel said, squinting her eyes. She sounded as if she didn't quite believe me.

"No."

She scrutinized me.

"Oh come on, you must feel something? How do you feel about it?" She wanted more.

"Like I said, it doesn't bother me. If two people love each other it doesn't make a difference if it's a man or a woman."

Noel looked at me and relief passed across her face. It was all so simple.

"Why did you come here?" I asked her. Maybe it was awkwardness of the conversation, but I thought again that Noel seemed out of place in this modern house, in this modern place, and incongruous.

"Well," Noel said, finally sitting back and relaxing. "If the mountain won't come to Mohammed, Mohammed must go to the mountain."

I looked at her. "What?" I didn't understand.

"For your mother," she said simply. "I came here to be with your mother."

I really didn't understand.

Chapter 42

Lily gave Noel the keys to her MG to teach me how to drive, hoping it would cheer her up. Her new life in California must have been at best disempowering, if not downright jarring. Life in France had been an interlude for Lily, an unsustainable fantasy or dream, and now here in California she was broke and drinking too much and not only that, Noel was sicker with her cancer. Lily was unable or seemingly unwilling to take this on. I was disenchanted as well, in that cruel and typical way that young people were with adult weakness and fallibility and just thought Noel was a fool to follow an alcoholic half around the world.

At any rate, my mother gave her the keys and instructed her to teach me how to drive. We headed out on the back roads of Malibu Canyon in the little sports car, a battered MG. Noel looked out at the dusty oaks and meadows of the Canyon, at the sagebrush and low-slung ranch houses and her face glazed over in a blank expression. It was as if she felt more foreign and alienated than ever, and was probably feeling sick as well. I looked sideways at her, jerking the car and jamming the gears and laughed, trying to snap her out of her mood. This was the place where I belonged, and then Noel laughed along and instructed me on how to press the clutch and change the gears.

I was in high school by then, back with my friends and had a new boyfriend, Lloyd, a senior at the school. It was an innocent relationship, contrary to what the adults thought; we never even kissed. We talked a lot and cut school and went swimming in Malibu Creek. And we got stoned on pot whenever his father wasn't in his house and listened to The Doors. Noel and I were near his house in the canyon.

"Have you heard of The Doors?" I said. I was driving the MG fast over a hill and it jumped off the ground and then skidded on gravel.

"What?"

"It's a band, a rock 'n' roll band."

Noel looked at me and then shook her head, no. She looked ill.

"Slow down!"

I looked over toward Lloyd's house to see if he was outside, and braked, slowing down. She told me how to change into a lower gear.

"Better?"

"Yes!" She forced a laugh.

She looked back out over the brown and yellow meadows, bleached from the sun, and that blank, sad look came back on her face, but I ignored it. I didn't want to think about it. I thought about the steep trail that led down to the swimming hole in Malibu Creek, and that Lloyd and I were going to cut school and go down there and go swimming. I was thinking about a gang of teenagers we had encountered there the first time we went there—the popular kids in his class— and that they were drinking beer and that Lloyd had said that they were lame and noisy and left beer cans by the creek, and that we were stoners and cool because we would just smoke pot and we didn't leave litter behind. I felt very confident, knowing that I loved this place and that it was my place, my home.

Noel looked over at me and she saw the satisfaction on my face, and she saw that I was somewhere else in my mind. Maybe she thought that I might prefer to have been somewhere else with someone else, and that she was somehow irrelevant to all this. Whatever it was, I could tell it depressed her.

I didn't see her too much after that, and when I did she never looked well; she seemed frailer every time. And pale. I always noticed how pale she looked. Yet at the same time she sparkled, Noel was evanescent. It was her personality; she loved life.

One of the last times that I saw her was at the Renaissance Fair. She was with Lily and another friend of Lily's and I was with Lloyd. We were making every effort to avoid the adults because we were stoned, but when we saw them it was too late, they saw us and came over. I was dressed in a brown leather fringe jacket and Lloyd was wearing a headband, hippy style. He was a handsome boy, rangy and dark with a pixyish face and warm brown eyes, and he was muscled from doing yard work. His father worked him hard clearing brush around his house. His straight brown hair was overgrown and held back from his face by the headband, and bleached orange blond on the ends from the sun. We were both beautiful and young.

The Fair was held up in the canyons behind LA, in grassy fields and oaks and people dressed in costumes wandered by. Lloyd and I were sitting on a hillside smoking a joint in the shade.

My mother spied us and came over to say hello. I could see she saw the joint.

"It's my mother," I said.

Lloyd quickly stubbed out the joint and jumped up. They stood there in front of us, Noel smiling and pale, pulled on the fringe of my jacket and said hello, and Lloyd good naturedly stumbled through his salutation. My mother pretended she hadn't seen the joint.

"He's cute," Noel said later, back at the house.

"You think so?"

"Uh huh. He's a good looking boy," she said, looking coy. "Do you like him?"

"Yeah," I said. I sounded completely non-committal. *Adults are so clueless.* I thought, and her coyness irritated me. We were just friends, and they just couldn't seem to grasp this and always insisted on making it more than it was.

"Yeah, I like him fine."

Maybe it was that she really wanted me to like boys, and the thing was Lloyd was gay and I was gay, and we didn't know it yet.

Chapter 43

"Where is Noel?" I asked. She had mysteriously and completely disappeared.

"She's at the City of Hope," my mother said.

"The City of Hope? What is that?" It sounded ominous.

"It's a hospital"

There was more.

"It's a hospital for cancer patients to go and die," Lily added.

"What? She's there alone?" This was too much, it was too sad.

"Yes," Lily nodded.

"Can I go to visit her? We should go to see her—"

"No." Lily shook her head.

"Have you been to visit her?" I heard my voice sounding stiff in reproach, and my face become stiff.

"She doesn't want me to," Lily said. "She doesn't want us to come there."

I just couldn't understand this. How could my mother let Noel be on her own at this time, to possibly face death? How could a person love someone and act this way? Was that love? I didn't think so.

"What happened to Noel?"

I didn't say the words out loud, the word "dead" was taboo, but I wanted to know, did Noel die at the City of Hope? There had been a silence about her.

"I told you, she went to the City of Hope."

"How did she get there?" I said and it sounded like an accusation. I needed to know the details.

"Where?"

Lily was playing dumb.

"To the City of Hope."

"I don't know," my mother said with a trace of irritation. "I sent her to my doctor and he referred her there." She sounded as if she was proud of her role in this, I noticed, as if this was enough.

"But how did she get there?"

"What do you mean?"

"How did she get to the City of Hope?"

"I don't know! I suppose she arranged some kind of ride."

I looked at my mother.

"She had an open sore on her breast," Lily said.

She died alone, I thought.

"She died there?"

"No, no, no," Lily said. "She left there. She didn't stay."

I was silent.

"She didn't stay there, she went back to Europe," Lily said. "She went back to France and then she moved to Algiers with Miriam."

"She did?"

Lily nodded. She had a familiar childlike look on her face that I recognized.

"I'm not responsible," Lily said. Her face was turned up in a saucy insouciant fashion when she made this announcement, her nose tilted slightly upward and she wasn't referring to Noel's situation in particular when she said this; it was more a general statement. Lily was a "free" spirit, free of responsibility and free of unwanted burdens. I glowered.

The thing is, Lily did love Noel. She was an active addict and she unable to be there for anyone at all. All I could feel was reproach that she wasn't there for Noel at the end. I saw it as a personal choice, a weakness and a failing, and the scary part of it was that Lily had been unable to be there for me either. I knew she loved Noel and that yes that she loved me as well, and that was the confounding and heart-breaking part of living with an alcoholic.

And Noel? To so blithely travel to America to be with Lily while knowing she was a drunk was just incomprehensible to me. Did she accept it, this inability on Lily's part to care for her when she needed it? I'll never know if she truly accepted it or had been secretly hoping for the best and had been let down in the worst kind of way.

Chapter 44

I imagined that the road to the City of Hope is lined with trees, neatly trimmed branches reaching up into the sky and falling away behind her line of vision as Noel traveled toward the gates of the hospital dead center on the horizon. And I imagined that a feeling of déjà vu had come over her as she traveled along, feeling her death was imminent and close , followed by sharp sadness and thoughts of my mother, Lily, and perhaps me, and her life in California.

She would pass through the gates to the City of Hope and see the clean buildings and elegant gardens and the nearness of her death might have become more sharply into focus and poignant, the California sunshine becoming brittle as she settled back in her seat trying to shake off dread. That's what it was—dread—and she might have realized then how much she didn't like this place, Los Angeles, and that she was out of her element and couldn't die here, that she wouldn't let it happen, that this place was a just a stopover.

Noel returned to Europe.

There was no home left in Haut de Cagnes, everyone had left. It had been a passing place and time in our life and Noel's life in the village. Cagnes had changed like so many places had changed, and so quickly it was gone by the time she went back. The village had become full of day-time tourists and the flats below built up with high-rises within a couple of years. The little fishing port disappeared.

Miriam had moved to North Africa to Algiers and Noel traveled there to be with her loyal friend, and Miriam was with her at her end. She had rented an apartment overlooking the sea in the European quarter, and when the time was right, and Noel's pain too great, Miriam administered an overdose of morphine and Noel quietly passed away.

The End

Also by Delaney Henderson

*****

The Travelers
A-Argus Books
ISBN 978-0981907574

*****

Travelers in foreign lands, especially the Middle East, are able to easily find drugs of every type for recreational use and for import-export. The magnificent sights of the Muslim community by day, conceal the behind-the-scenes activities of the night. Out there are the "Users," who want to capitalize on the lucrative markets of the United States and its neighbors.

The lure of easy money and the icy thrill of breaking all the rules prove to be a virtually irresistible attraction to young American tourists and their counterparts around the world.

The combination of free access to copious amounts of drugs, sex, danger and excitement lead travelers to taste the forbidden fruits and encourages them to partake in the chase of modern ecstasy; sometimes with fatal results.

Young Americans, French hippies, Canadian drug smugglers, home bound Muslim woman… travelers. Fast friends and close bonds are made in a time and place when it was more possible, pre 9/11. These people are eager and open to know about the lives of the people around them, people from different cultures. They gather in the cafes and hotels of Casa Blanca, they get high on hashish, they explore the city, and most importantly they get to know one another. Inevitably as these young people move into adulthood they meet their respective fates, predetermined by virtue of where they are born.

~*~*~

www.ingramcontent.com/pod-product-compliance
Lightning Source LLC
Chambersburg PA
CBHW051537260626
47170CB00003B/977